P9-CRG-267

Praise for
JONATHAN MILES
and
DEAR AMERICAN AIRLINES

"A fine first novel . . . emotionally rewarding."
— RICHARD RUSSO, *New York Times Book Review*

"Deliciously cynical . . . allows Miles to riff on everything from 9/11 and middle-age malaise to toilet-stall graffiti and the gecko in Geico commercials, while slyly moving his hero toward something of an epiphany." —*Washington Post*

"Miles is such a clever, amusing writer that he turns what should be shtick into a terrifically fun read." —*Boston Globe*

"There are a few simple rules for writing an effective letter of complaint. Keep it simple and straightforward. Never apologize. Include a possum-trapping scene. And always make it novel-length. Anyone can do this, but only Jonathan Miles can also make it boozy and profane, honest to the glorious wretched bone, and beautiful, just beautiful."
—JOHN HODGMAN, author of *The Areas of My Expertise*

"The writing reminded me of brilliant, early-days Martin Amis—except with redemption and hope. It's not easy to write a book this good."
—ELIZABETH GILBERT, author of *Eat, Pray, Love*

"Hilariously vitriolic." —*Harper's Bazaar*

DEAR AMERICAN AIRLINES

Dear American Airlines

Jonathan Miles

MARINER BOOKS

HOUGHTON MIFFLIN HARCOURT

Boston • New York

First Mariner Books edition 2009
Copyright © 2008 by Jonathan Miles

www.hmhbooks.com

Library of Congress Cataloging-in-Publication Data
Miles, Jonathan.
Dear American Airlines / Jonathan Miles.
p. cm.
ISBN 978-0-547-05401-8
1. Air travel—Fiction. 2. Introspection—Fiction. I. Title.
PS3613.I5322D43 2008
813'.6—dc22   2007052150
ISBN 978-0-547-23790-9 (PBK.)

Book design by Melissa Lotfy

PRINTED IN THE UNITED STATES OF AMERICA

DOC 10 9 8 7 6 5 4

Excerpts from "Casida de la Mujer Tendida"/"Casida of the Reclin-
ing Woman" by Federico García Lorca © Herederos de Federico García
Lorca from *Obras Completas* (Galaxia/Gutenberg, 1996 edition). Translation by W.S. Merwin © W.S. Merwin and Herederos de Federico García
Lorca. All rights reserved. For information regarding rights and permis-
sions, please contact lorca@artslaw.co.uk or William Peter Kosmas, Esq.,
8 Franklin Square, London W14 9UU.

"Lost in Translation" by James Merrill, from *Collected Poems.* Copyright © 1976 by James Merrill. Used by permission of Alfred A. Knopf, a
division of Random House, Inc.

"The Prelude" by Jacek Gutorow, translated by David Kennedy and
Jacek Gutorow. From *Linia Zycia*, published by Wydawnictwo Znak.
Copyright © 2006 by Jacek Gutorow. Used by permission of the author.

in memoriam

LARRY BROWN

(1951–2004)

bro

DEAR AMERICAN AIRLINES

Dear American Airlines,

My name is benjamin r. ford and I am writing to request a refund in the amount of $392.68. But then, no, scratch that: *Request* is too mincy & polite, I think, too officious & Britishy, a word that walks along the page with the ramrod straightness of someone trying to balance a walnut on his upper ass cheeks. Yet what am I saying? Words don't have ass cheeks! Dear American Airlines, I am rather *demanding* a refund in the amount of $392.68. Demanding demanding demanding. In Italian, *richie-dere. Verlangen* in German and требовать in the Russki tongue but you doubtless catch my drift. Imagine, for illustrative purposes, that there's a table between us. Hear that sharp sound? That's me slapping the table. Me, Mr. Payable to Benjamin R. Ford, whapping the damn legs off it! Ideally you're also imagining concrete walls and a naked lightbulb dangling above us: Now picture me bursting to my feet and kicking the chair behind me, with my finger in your face and my eyes all red and squinty and frothy bittles of spittle freckling the edges of my mouth as I bellow, roar, yowl, as I blooooow like the almighty mother of all blowholes: *Give me my goddamn money back!* See? Little twee *request* doesn't quite capture it, does it? Nossir. This is a *demand*. This is fucking serious.

Naturally I'm aware that ten zillion cranks per annum make

1

such demands upon you. I suppose you little piglets are accustomed to being huffed upon and puffed upon. Even now, from my maldesigned seat in this maldesigned airport, I spy a middle-aged woman waving her arms at the ticket counter like a sprinklerhead gone awry. Perhaps she is serious, too. Maybe, like me, even *fucking* serious. Yet the briefcase by the woman's feet and her pleated Talbots suit lead me to conclude that she's probably missing some terribly important meeting in Atlanta where she's slated to decide something along the lines of which carbonated beverage ten zillion galoots aged 18–34 will drink during a specified half-hour of television viewing in four to six midwestern markets and I'm sure the ticket agent is being sweetly sympathetic to the soda lady's problem but screw her anyway. So a half-zillion galoots drink Pepsi rather than Coke, so what? My entire being, on the other hand, is now dust on the carpet, ripe and ready to be vacuumed up by some immigrant in a jumpsuit.

Please calm down sir, I can hear you saying. Might we recommend a healthy snack, perhaps some sudoku? Yes, sudoku: apparently the analgesic *du jour* of the traveling class. That little game is what appears to be getting my fellow citizens through these hours of strandedness, hours that seem to be coagulating, wound-like, rather than passing. They say a watched pot never boils but baby it's tough not to watch when you're neck-deep in the pot. Just how many hours so far, I can't say—not with any precision anyway. Why are there so few clocks in airports? You can't turn your head more than ten degrees in a train station without hitting another clock on the wall, the ceiling, the floor, etc. You'd think that the smartasses who design airports, taking a hint from their forebears, would think to hang a clock or two on the walls instead of leaving the time-telling to the digital footnotes at the bottom of the scattered schedule screens. I take an oversized amount of pride in the fact that I've never worn a wristwatch since my thirteenth birthday when my father gave me a Timex and I smashed it with a nine-iron to see how much licking would stop its ticking (not much, as it turned out). But then airports weren't designed for people like me, a fact becoming more and more obvious as I divide my present between smoking cigarettes on the sidewalk outside and drumming my fingers on the armrests of the chairs inside. But even more odious than the clocklessness, I might add, is replacing the *beep-beep-beep* of those passenger carts with digitized birdsong imitations. Birdsongs! I shouldn't have to tell you that being run down by a twelve-foot sparrow is little improvement over being run down by a militarized golfcart. But then that's a matter for the smartasses, not you, so mea culpa. We must be choosy with our battles, or so I've been told.

It occurs to me that none of this will do me a bit of good unless I state my particulars, to wit: My ticket—purchased for $392.68 as I've relevantly aforementioned and will continue to mention, as frequently as a tapdancer's clicks—is for round-trip passage from New York–LaGuardia to Los Angeles's LAX (with a forty-five-minute layover at Chicago O'Hare; were there a clock nearby, I'd divulge the truer length of my layover, but it's safe to say it's edging toward eight hours, with no end in sight). In that eightish-hour period I've smoked seventeen cigarettes which wouldn't be notable save for the fact that the dandy Hudson News outlets here don't stock my brand so I'll soon be forced to switch to another, and while that shouldn't upset me it does. In fact, it enrages me. Here's my life in dangly tatters and I can't even enjoy this merest of my pleasures. Several hours ago a kid in a Cubs windbreaker bummed one of mine and I swear if I spy him again I'll smash him like a Timex. Cough it up, you turd. But then all this talk of smoking is giving me the familiar itch, so if you'll excuse me for a moment I'm off to the sidewalk, as required by law, to scratch it.

- - - -

THERE NOW, ALL BETTER. Oops, except that I'm not. Of late I've been suffering weird pains in my lower back and these airport chairs with their gen-u-ine Corinthian Naugahyde upholstery are only aggravating the pain. Throughout my life I vowed I would never be the sort of geezer reduced to conversing about nothing save his health maladies. This was until the day I developed maladies of my own to converse about. Truly, they're endlessly fascinating and impossible to keep to oneself! How can you talk about anything else when your physical being is disintegrating, when you can feel everything below your neck going steadily *kaput?* You certainly wouldn't think of discussing, say, Lacanian theory on a jumbo jet spiraling earthward. Unless of course you were Lacan, but even then: Jeez, Jacques, call the kiddos. Back when I was drinking I tended to ignore my bodily malfunctions—full disclosure: During the later dark years of my drinking, I tended to ignore even my bodily *functions*—but now they've become a kind of hobby for me. I fill my private hours with tender proddings and pokings of my interior organs, in the manner of old women in *babushkas* examining mushy supermarket peaches. Plus there's the time I spend online Googling my various symptoms. Do you know that the first diagnosis the internet will offer you for any symptom is almost always a venereal disease? This must be causing acute distress for those hypochondriacal members of our society allowing their genitals to mingle. In the seventh grade the rumor was that your willy would drop clean off if you tugged on it too much (or put it inside a black girl, an indicia of the cultural clime of mid-'60s New Orleans) which caused me infinite grief and worry. The thought of running to my mother with my unfastened manhood in one hand was enough to put me off onanism for several years. The horror! My mother was a crafty sort who doubtlessly would have tried to reattach the poor thing via the aid of a hot glue gun, some sewing thread, glitter, and cut-out photographs from *National Geographic,* making my private parts look like an elementary school project about orangutans. "There now," she would've said. "All better."

My mother will be seventy-three next month. I mention this fact since it's not just me, Mr. Payable to Benjamin R. Ford, who is presently out that $392.68 you charged us—due to the current configuration of my life, me and Miss Willa are victims in this together. Mug me, you mug my ma. Ya dirty mugs. Because she suffered a debilitating stroke three years ago, I take care of Miss Willa with the aid of a twenty-seven-year-old dumpling of a girl from the Polish countryside named Aneta who also from time to time assists me with my translations. All this, mind you, within the confines of the 2BR, third-story apt. in the West Village that I've called home since Bush the Elder was president. Back then it provided me elbowroom galore. Now, with my mother shuffling about and Aneta galumphing after her, my waking and sleeping hours are primarily squashed together into one room—a Balzacian garret fitted with a desk, books, and a sofa that folds out into a bed but only if you push the desk against the wall each night. It ain't pretty but we manage.

The stroke may have been the best thing that could have happened to my mother. No doubt this sounds beastly, especially considering that she cannot move the right side of her body and must communicate by scrawling pithy comments on one of the multicolored Post-it pads she keeps piled on her lap, but my mother used to be crazy and now she is not. I don't mean crazy like your old Aunt Edna who's still dancing the tango at eighty and makes uncomfortably blue comments at the Thanksgiving dinner table. I mean manic-depressive schizophrenic crazy, the hard stuff. During a stroke, parts of the brain are starved of oxygen and die, and in the case of my mother, apparently the crazy parts got starved. The stroke cleaved her in two but, hooray and I mean it, left the good half functioning. This isn't to suggest that things are hunky-dory at home but rather to say that things were once worse. To be honest things were once terrible but then that's another story and you're probably skimming already.

Dear American Airlines, do you even read all these letters you must receive? I imagine them funneling into a giant bin in a sorting room in some warehouse set out in a dancefloor-flat stretch of Texas plain, mounds and mounds of stamped envelopes from all corners of this vast republic, handwritten and typewritten and some scribbled in Crayola crayon, questions and pleas and suggestions and rants and maybe even mash notes from easily sated dinkums who *lurved* the Cincinnati travel tips in the in-flight magazine. Or maybe they're all emails now, unpunctuated, misspelled, flecked with emoticons, sizzling through a grand nest of wires before landing, with a digital ping, inside some doublewide trailer-sized mainframe computer. Back in my very early twenties I actually wrote a thank-you note to the Swisher Cigar Co. of Jacksonville, Fla., to express my gratitude for the sublime if stinky cheer its flagship brand then provided me. I spent an inordinate amount of time crafting that letter and went so far as to cite for particular praise the Swisher Sweet's "cognac-and-campfire aroma." That I'd never caught so much as a whiff of cognac by that time mattered little; it was alliterative, and alliteration bewitched me to such an extent that in my undergraduate years I romanced, in succession, a Mary Mattingly, a Karen Carpenter (not the singer), a Patricia Powell, and a Laura Lockwood, as if culling my dates straight from the pages of a comic book. I remember being bitterly disappointed by the Swisher Cigar Co.'s response to my letter: A coupon for a free box that arrived without even the merest personal acknowledgment of my note. Sure, the coupon came in handy, but really. You have to be careful about trying to make connections in this world, or so I learned.

Aneta helped me pick out the necktie for my trip west.

Why I would trust an Eastern European girl whose wardrobe is founded primarily on Mickey Mouse t-shirts in varying colors including poop brown is beyond me, except that I think I liked having a female opinion on the matter, since the reasons for my trip — the trip you are currently thwarting, fuck you very much — are entirely female. And I do mean entirely. My daughter is getting married tomorrow, though I'm not sure "married" is the correct & legal term since she's quote-unquote marrying another woman. This came as quite the surprise to me though I confess that, at the time I learned of it, any news from my daughter would have been classified as surprising. She's engaged to a woman named Sylvana, meaning my future daughter-in-law is one letter away from being kin to my television set. I don't know if Stella — that's my daughter, named after her mother — will be the bride or the groom and I suspect it's poor form for me to inquire. And how does a father assess his daughter's choice of spouse when it's another girl? I generally know a beer-guzzling, wife-beating, underbathed, unemployable lout when I see one, unless she's wearing a dress in which case it's damnably hard to tell. Sylvana is a lawyer which should be a comfort — oh goody, my daughter's marrying a lawyer! — but that's about as much as I know about her. Of course, I don't know much about Stella, either. Her mother and I split up a long time ago and for complicated or possibly uncomplicated reasons I faded almost completely out of her life: an old story, right, the father as vanishing taillight. The last photograph I have of her is from her high school graduation, and came to me not from either of my Stellas but directly from the Sears Portrait Studio, as if they (the Stellas, maybe Sears) were legally obligated to send me a print. The photograph shook in my hands when I received it because Stella's resemblance to her mother was total and precise, and the venom of that union's crash still lingers in my arteries, still buzzes my tongue with a chemical aftertaste. Staring at my daughter's portrait was like viewing the evidence of a long-ago crime. Look: I don't deny I was once an ogre. What's harder and more painful for me to gauge is if I'm still one. Yet, humbly, I consider the necktie in my luggage a hopeful sign. That is, if you nitwits haven't gone and lost it.

DEAR AMERICAN AIRLINES, permit me to introduce Walenty Mozelewski, who, by dint of dark coincidence, is having transportation snarls of his own. Walenty should be on his way home to Poland (via England, for his discharge) from the war, having fought with the Polish II Corps at the Battle of Monte Cassino (Italy), where he lost his left leg to the combined efforts of a mortar shell and an overworked Swiss combat surgeon. Quite the ordeal, and I'm afraid the shellshock has muddied his brain. He boarded the wrong train and is now on his way to Trieste. This should be a mere inconvenience but Walenty cannot help wondering what would happen if he stepped off the train in Trieste and never in all his life boarded another. It would be like death without the dying, is what he's thinking: the loss of everything—his wife, his two children, his home, his former job as a factory clerk in a factory that makes parts for other factories—the loss of it all, save his breath and his memories. Poor Walenty! He's staring through the window at the winter outside, fogging the glass with his exhalations. Listen:

> Every few minutes or so there appeared a house or houses outside, most at the ends of narrow, lonely, low-walled roads, some of the houses half-ruined and ice-chinked but others with gray tendrils of smoke rising from their stone chimneys and a faint yellow glow visible from inside them. Walenty wondered who lived in those houses, and what

they would do if a one-legged soldier came to their door and asked if he could stay for the night and, if that was fine, then perhaps forever. Or how the soldier would be able to tell which house might be Heaven and which might be Hell, if either they were.

Those last sentences are awkward, I know. But here's the caveat: I haven't actually started translating yet—this is my initial read-through, and since you'll recall that I'm presently stranded in an airport without access to (a) my reference books, and (b) my beloved Lucky Strikes, I hope I'll be excused for flying by the seat of my pants here. (Flying! What a concept. I'd like to do more of it.)

The author's name is Alojzy Wojtkiewicz, and the title is *The Free State of Trieste*. This is the third novel of Alojzy's I've translated, and he's likely to provide me as much help on this one as he has all the others: by which I mean, not squat. He tends to treat me (as he apparently does all his translators) like the new husband of a wife he's ditched: Yes, he'll field a few questions, and perhaps mutter some wan advice, but really: She's your problem now, *kumpel*. Not that I'm bellyaching, mind you. We translators must be realistic. To translate a literary work is to make love to a woman who will always be in love with someone else. You can ravish her, worship her, even ruin her; but she'll never be yours to possess. Less romantically, I've sometimes thought of translation as being akin to cooking. At your disposal is the meat of an animal, and it's up to you to create dishes from it, to make it digestible. But the novelist or poet has the more Godly job. He gets to create the animal.

I met Alojzy twenty years ago when we shared a duplex studio at an artists' colony up in Idaho, back when I was scamming delicious fellowships for the third-rate poems I was writing. (You would be appalled at the amount of state & federal taxpayer money—i.e. grants, fellowships, other assorted poet subsidies—that went into my pockets over the years, especially if you did a cost-benefit analysis of the poetry it yielded. Though, wait: Aren't you the proud recipient of something like ten kazillion dollars in federal bailout funds? Well then, lookee here at us. Flightless birds of a feather.) Every day at noon the colony's cook would deliver us lunches, and Alojzy and I would sit out on the deck and eat our turkey sandwiches and apples while staring at the Boulder Mountains and then we would chainsmoke and talk about women before retreating back into our studios, where Alojzy finished his second novel and where I took vodka-fueled "naps" between bouts of additional chainsmoking. Back then he was swarthy and thick-muscled, with a square head and torso that made him resemble a piece of Mission furniture; going by his more recent author photos, the last two decades have seen Alojzy progressively swaddling himself in fat, a hard square gone soft and circular. From a distance you might mistake him for a honeybun. This is to be expected, however. When I met him he had just ended a several-year stint as a bricklayer; these days, his primary physical activity seems to be signing his name to leftist petitions with one hand while gripping a half-gnawed sparerib in the other.

But I digress. My aim here was to acquaint you with Walenty, since, for the moment, he seems to be all I have in the world, but I veered into some related humbuggeries and lost track of him. Sigh. Nonetheless, I'm afraid you'll have to permit me my digressions. Digressing, after all, is not so different from rerouting, and let's not pretend, dear ones, that you're innocent of that.

DEAR AMERICAN AIRLINES, since when did you start canceling flights in midair? The plane from New York to Chicago was one of those "streamlined" contraptions roughly the size and shape of an econo-model dildo. We circled O'Hare for an hour before the pilot informed us he was landing in Peoria. Peoria! In my youth I thought Peoria was a fictional place that Sherwood Anderson and Sinclair Lewis had cooked up one night at the tail end of a gin bender. But no, it exists. We sat on the runway for more than an hour before a handsome pilot with exquisitely parted hair emerged to tell us that the flight was "officially canceled." Wha? But he offered us all a bus ride to O'Hare "on the house," kind soul that he was, the revealing of which I hope won't endanger his job. Not that I'd worry too much about him: Go ahead and can him, he has a guaranteed second career as a JCPenney catalog model. The (alleged) cause for this fuckedupedness was (allegedly) foul weather blowing off Lake Michigan but after eight-plus hours in Chicago I can tell you, without a pinch of hesitation, that the weather here is flat-out delightful and you're more than welcome to visit for a round of golf to so verify. Pack some sunscreen.

Yet all around me this nation's stranded folk are badgering ticket agents, muffling their children's whining by stuffing the local variety of hot dogs into their small mouths, checking and rechecking their watches, and, most of all, inexhaustibly bitching into cellphones. Every now and then I walk twenty yards or so to check the schedule screens. I'm not alone in this chore but I do seem to be the only one unequipped with a cellphone. No big shakes there, as I've already made my one call—it didn't go so well—and I'm anyway loyal to payphones. I stand beneath the screens like a child waiting for Santa's sleigh to appear in the night sky, examining each star for the faintest trace of movement, ears overattuned to the jingle of far-off bells. But the screens barely flicker. All flights westward canceled, eastward canceled, everything canceled. The sky above us one giant fermata, an interminable chord lying wounded in the middle of a song, a deadening hollow thrummmmm

----

STELLA IS PROBABLY laughing about this. Stella the elder, I mean. Not a happy, lilting laugh: no, more like an acidic, I-told-you-so laugh, as in *hahaha once an asshole always an asshole haha . . . ha.* The sort of laugh that's sometimes mistaken for a cough or a cancer symptom. Did I mention she was beautiful once? Well, she was. Like the leading lady from a Bogart flick, so I thought back then, with a finely sculpted aristocrat's jaw and eyes as deep, blue, and cold as the North Atlantic glimpsed through a submarine's porthole. The thin lips of a killer and a long narrow ivory neck. A demure chocolate mole on her inner thigh that I blithely befriended. Would it still remember me? Hard to believe that it, at least, wouldn't welcome me home: Hello darlin'. In our lazy postcoital tangles I swear I used to *breathe* Stella, as if inhaling her aerosolized essence, trying to flood my lungs with her. Surely you remember what that's like: lying there in the wet dark, unafraid for the first time in your life, drenched in a balmy peace, content to die. But then, stop, it's useless and mawkish to dwell on such things, right-rightright. Buck up, Bennie. So every tomato has its soft spot, big whoop. You were young like everyone else. Quit making mountains out of moles.

It happened like this: I was twenty-four, she twenty-seven. I'd dropped out of grad school the year before to embark upon a career in romantic dissolution, spending nine- and ten-hour daily stretches in a narrow, gummy cockpit of an Uptown New Orleans bar called Billy Barnes' Turf Exchange. The Exchange, for short, and goddamn what a saloon: ancient coonass bruisers drinking away disability checks, weird old frilly bats from the neighborhood sipping Chambord or Campari, off-duty line cooks and oyster shuckers, displaced hippies, slumming Tulane kids, greasy pool sharks, a cigar-smoking Rottweiler named Punch, Seersucker Bob who never wore anything but, Skee-zacks who used his trumpet as a beer bong, Dead Fred whose ashes were behind the bar, Spud, Pete the Spy, Al the Horny

Wheelchair Homo, Bum's Breath Mike (B. B. Mike for short), Crazy Jane, me too. Our ringmaster was Felix, the owner, a doughy, hairless connoisseur of dirty jokes and fry-batter who would take out his false teeth for a dollar. He called himself Felix the Fat so we did the same. Tuesday was Ladies' Night, the only night Felix would spring for a band, and there'd be so many halter tops a-bouncing on the dancefloor that you felt like you were inside a lottery ball machine. But those nights were the exception. Mostly it was a dim, garrulous joint, filled with neighborhood steadies and worn chatter and smogged with tobacco smoke and cuss words, as comfortable, rank, and beloved as the ratty old pair of house slippers you slide on to fetch the morning news. How I adored it! Back then I was broke, sloshed, undernourished, unwashed, intermittently suicidal, but more generally, and sometimes rhapsodically, happy as hell: what the French call *l'extase langoureuse*, the ecstasy of languishing.

Stella was the cool opposite: sharp, ambitious, level, metrical, severe. An aspiring poet like me, though the style & substance of her poems were the obverse of mine. When we met I was coediting a small doomed lit journal called *Rag and Bone Shop* and she'd just started work on her master's at Tulane. My coeditor's apartment on Magazine Street—his name was Charles Ford; everyone assumed we were brothers—doubled as the *R&BS* offices, and it was there, at one of the parties we always threw after picking the issues up from the printer, that Stella and I met. We'd published two of her poems in that edition of *R&BS*—one about a quilt, sort of, and the other, very literally, about a bottlecap crucifix. It was the former poem that intrigued me, because it ended with a scene of a woman having sex atop her great-grandmother's hand-stitched quilt, "staining it with creation," which struck me as a lovely and vaguely kinky line and made me curious about its author.

Her hair was braided that night and she was wearing a blousy silk shirt and bluejeans. On the hi-fi: Nick Lowe, the Specials, the Buzzcocks, Ian Dury & the Blockheads. A baroque glass bong circling the kitchen and a local medievalist performing a second line on his way to the potty. We ended up on Charles's balcony overlooking Magazine, Stella and I, sitting on a porch swing with our feet propped on the balcony rail, bubbly drunk. What did we talk about? Who knows. The dis-and-dat of two creatures commencing a mating dance. Crazy mothers (ah, she had one too). James Merrill. Time travel. A shared fondness for neon. My enigmatic coeditor, her downblouse-peering old roach of a thesis advisor. Oh, and yes, I learned she'd never set foot inside the Exchange! Gallantly, I promised to take her. Later, while we were kissing, I opened my eyes to the sight of Charles's naked pale rump pressed flat against the window. From inside I could hear him singing, "When da moon hiz your eye . . . ," and so on and so forth.

We were the last to leave the party. Inside we found Charles passed out openmouthed on his couch, and after carefully sliding down his boxers and finding a marker, we wrote a poem on his ass: *Roses are red / violets are blue / with my buttocks so white / I bid you goodnight.* (Stella would later disavow her participation in this act, citing it as one of the early missed clues of my unsuitability as husband, father, gentleman, etc., but I vividly remember her right thumb curled around the elastic of Charles's boxers, and the brutal glee she seemed to be stifling, because I was surprised [and aroused] by the sexual birr she brought to the task, the way her involvement tipped it, from boozy conception up to the moment we began writing, from frathouse-style prank to dark-edged violation . . . anyway, she denies it.) Downstairs on the sidewalk I kissed Stella some more—those cliffhanger kisses, you know, when you feel as if you'll drop to your doom if your tongues untwine—before she sank into the seat of her car and disappeared. Then I stood there for a long while, my heart a sparkler spraying light across the sidewalk.

YET I'M VEERING off-point once again, aren't I? French-style kisses & whatnot, kerphooey. Dear American Airlines, I apologize. Please understand that these are not the best of times. Outside, by the luggage porters, an elderly woman who was smoking beside me just told me the most dismal of tales: Her husband suffered a "coronary" while driving and plunged his Fiat off a central California cliff but thanks to his seatbelt was saved from dying and was instead reduced to a vegetative state now going on four years. His dear munchkin of a wife sits with him for six hours a day waiting for the random blink of an eyelid that will return him to the mammalian. As she told me this she dug a packet of Kleenex out of her fannypack which I presumed was for her—that story awarded her the right to shed tears—but which she offered to me. I've never been adept at keeping my heart from advertising itself on my sleeve, and I guess I was wearing that wounded, onion-stink expression to which I'm prone. I started to decline the gift but she was rifling through her fannypack for something else. I was hoping it wouldn't be a still-life photo of her ventilated, intubated husband because that risked provoking a fit of blubbering from me. Instead it was a little machine resembling an overweight BlackBerry phone which she explained was a handheld slot machine. This was what kept her sane, she told me, and urged me to take a few spins—in the "virtual" sense, of course—which I did. A cherry, a seven, and what looked like a lemon! Two sevens and a cherry! Loss and more loss. The munchkin said all life requires of us, "by George," is to find one reason a day to go on. Besides playing the little video slot machine, she said, she makes sure to always have something coming in the mail such as a sweater from L.L.Bean or a new garden trowel from Smith & Hawken. To always be expecting. Before heading back inside—"I hear they're running short on cots for us strandees," she said—she told me the Kleenex was mine and advised me to keep my upper lip stiff. Followed literally this advice tends to make one appear on the brink of a sneeze but nevermind the literal. The old woman gave me her tissues and I'm doing what she says.

MIND IF WE CHECK IN with Walenty? For just a minute or two while my lip holds sdiff like dis. Here he is on page 17, having just stepped off the train in Trieste:

> He was unprepared for the raw color of it all. For three years he had seen no color except for the beef-red of wounds and crimson splashes of blood; everything else had been painted in hard, parched shades of gray and brown and black. Mud, gunmetal, rust, smoke, night, char, concertina wire, shovels, ash, corpse-skin, fog, mortar shells, bones, the sharp-ribbed mongrels that cowered growling behind rubble piles. Stepping off the train now, however, was like passing through a rainbow. The station itself, yellow like a daisy, was charged with color: here the gaudy flash of summer silks, there the rose-colored fringe of a woman's drawstring purse, here the phosphorescent gloss of a businessman's navy suit, and strewn across the waxed floors were the salmon-hued confetti of discarded tickets.

("Confetti": a tiny liberty that I'm taking. Alojzy has it as *świąteczne odpadki*, which translated literally means "festive trash." But what trash is more festive than confetti? Ah, the pinprick joys of translating. Anyway, onward . . .)

> Walenty's eyes stung him, and he nearly lost his breath. Save for the few Kiwi soldiers posted in the corners, and the

deadness of his false foot as his shoe scraped the floor, there was nothing to suggest that the war had been anything but a sour nightmare.

He sat down at a table in a café inside the station and, still dizzy and overwhelmed, held the table edge to steady himself. The young girl who came to take his order was dark-haired, with tanned glossy skin, and the pureness of her expression—a mix of boredom, dreaminess, and tender ignorance—made clear to him that she had lost nothing in life, not yet. He noticed a small, fish-shaped scar on her elbow: probably from a childhood fall. No doubt she had cried—the grating, screechy cries he'd associated with children before he went to war, before he'd heard what children are capable of. Deep howls of total vacuumed loss.

"Do you have coffee?" he asked.

"Yes," she said.

"*Surrogato?*"

"No. Coffee."

"Please, then. A cup."

When she returned to deliver his coffee, he noticed her lingering and staring shyly at his prosthetic leg, at his exposed mechanical ankle. His eyes caught hers. "Does it hurt?" she asked finally.

"No," he said. "It doesn't hurt. Not anymore. It just reminds me of hurt. Like a memory that sits right in the front of your brain and can't be budged or extinguished." He did not want to drive her off, to have her think he was a melancholy cripple, the cliché of the wounded soldier, so he smiled. His smile, however, was lopsided and awkward, as if the muscles of his jaw had forgotten their old routine. He hoped it hadn't seemed a leer.

She nodded inscrutably and went off to service other tables. When she returned he ordered another cup, and when she brought it to him he said, "Do you know what's strange?" She waited, so he went on: "In my dreams I always have two legs. I think that's the worst part. Every morning, after dreaming, I awaken a full man. But then I reach down and feel my false leg and everything that happened to me happens all over again, in that instant, as though every day I am losing my leg and my comrades for the first time. That's the worst part. I dream backwards."

He did not expect the girl to smile at this, but she did. Lightly, she said, "You need new dreams," as if it was self-evident, as if he had said he was hungry and she'd recommended food. She'd made it sound simple.

It's *not* simple, of course, but you certainly can't blame Walenty for hoisting his hopes up. How pleasant to think of the past as something curable, as a benign rather than malignant cancer, no? Almost as pleasant a concept as a world in which tickets costing $392.68 earned you passage to your destination on the date printed on the ticket. But just as goddamn unlikely.

- - - -

SINCE WE'RE SORT OF on the subject of hindsight, dear American Airlines, why don't we discuss how this mess could have been avoided? We won't bother with your official excuse of rotten weather because I've plainly unmasked that one with my frequent measuring of the climate outside, which, at last check, showed a mix of cool and pleasant with a ninety percent chance of continued pleasantness developing through the morning, with winds, like your flight schedules, light and variable. So talk to me. Did banal old greed induce you to overschedule your flights, à la bank robbers unable to stop stuffing their bags despite the wails of nearing sirens? (Peek into that corner office. Do you see fat men eyeing your national route map while twirling handlebar mustaches? Then the answer is probably yes.) Or do you plan so tightly and rigidly that the delay of one plane in, say, Dallas can cause a monumental backup akin to a stalled tractor-trailer on the George Washington Bridge at

8:30 A.M.? Or, similarly, are airlines like yourself susceptible to something like the Butterfly Effect, so that the delay caused by a pickled passenger trying to board an early-morning flight in Ibiza can provoke a chain reaction, with delay piling upon delay, and then cancellation upon cancellation, until poor Chicago O'Hare—the sacrificial goat of air travel—is shut down completely? If that's the case, maybe I'm being too hard on you. Perhaps my beef is actually with Señor Fabio Eurotrash who rolled off a foam-strewn Ibiza dancefloor at six A.M. with sixteen Red-Bull-and-vodkas still fizzing in his gut and whose clumsy pre-takeoff attempt at self-fellatio in Seat 3A forced an interminable delay while his pretzeled ass was removed from the plane. But then why stop there? The beauty of hindsight is that it's infinite. After all, you could reasonably if acidly retort that this entire hash is my fault because twenty years ago I flushed my life down the toilet. Zing! Good one, AA. Or, stepping further back, that it's Willa Desforge's fault for letting a disconsolate-eyed Polack impregnate her one unairconditioned night midcentury in New Orleans. Ouch, sucker-punch! Funny thing is, though, Miss Willa would agree with you on that one. If she could somehow connect the dots, my mother would fix the blame for everything from Pol Pot to global warming to the undarned holes in her socks on that one humid unguarded night that was the end of her and the beginning of me.

And it began, truth to tell, with a possum. Sit tight, I have a story to tell. Apparently we have time.

Miss Willa Desforge met Henryk Gniech at her parents' home on South Tonti Street in 1953 courtesy of, yessir, a possum: a fat, spooked creature with mottled fur that was neither gray nor brown nor white but a splotchy and disheveled mixture of the three, and with a long fleshy tail almost obscene in its nude pinkness. The possum had taken up residence in the attic directly above Miss Willa's bedroom, and, despite weeks of grumbly and intermittent efforts, my grandfather, a trust and estate attorney for a white-shoe Uptown firm, had been incapable of banishing it from the house. So one Saturday morning he borrowed the neighbor's ladder and patched every hole and rotted edge of the roof soffits and fascias with scrap wood and squares of rumpled aluminum, barring (he thought) any further access by the possum. But possums are nocturnal, so instead of watching my grandfather seal the attic from up in a tree or behind a trashcan, as Gerald Desforge, Esq., imagined, the possum watched from *inside* the dark attic as the specks of infiltrating sunlight steadily disappeared from its lair, like stars fizzling to black in the night sky. That evening, beginning just after twilight and lasting deep into the wee hours, the Desforges were treated to an unusually raucous performance on the ceiling above Miss Willa's bed: scritches, scratches, hyperagitated scurries. "It's trapped and it's frantic," my mother said, but my grandfather was unsympathetic. "It will be over soon enough," he said. "How long can it last up there?"

Longer than one might expect or endure, as it turned out. Every night, for a full week, my mother stared stiffly and sleeplessly at the ceiling while the possum launched escape attempt after escape attempt, clawing at the aluminum and gnawing at the wood, and every night the weight of its suffering seemed to sink heavier and heavier upon her in that bed, like a deadening cloak of blame . . . a guilt quilt.

Of course, to fully understand the situation, you need to know something about my mother at the time. Miss Willa Desforge was an outlandishly beautiful girl, with startling green eyes and hair as black and glistening as a newly waxed hearse, as well as a gifted painter admitted to the John McCrady Art School at the age of twelve and, at fifteen, as a special student to Sophie Newcomb College's art school. But God does not bestow that kind of beauty and talent freely, as you know or should know; His love must be paid. For my mother, the price

He exacted was schizophrenia, diagnosed at sixteen following her first suicide attempt.

She'd always had delusions of grandeur (and does to this day, nevermind the indignities of Post-it notes and spoon-feeding); this is partly owing to my grandparents, who coddled their only child insufferably—their Willa was the sole survivor of three pregnancies, sandwiched between two stillborn siblings—and instilled in my mother the belief, with an alarmingly literal precision, that she was an angel Providence had conferred upon them to raise. Invisible wings, supernatural faculties, a heart bleached of sin, the whole warped works. But at sixteen she began to fear the world was tilting against her—that, grabby and envious, it longed to strip her of her wings. First she noticed greasy fingerprints on her bedsheets, too faint for others to see, but clearly, to her, the black smeary evidence that somebody or somebodies had it in for her. Cribbing from her Nancy Drew books, she dusted her room for more fingerprints, and, with openmouthed horror, discovered them everywhere: on her nightstand, inside her dresser drawers, freckling the walls, and, most disturbingly, strewn across her body. Made visible (to her) by the dusting of talcum powder, they were like bruises as seen in a photo negative: whorls of white on her legs, arms, and shoulders, and ringing her neck like a pearl choker. My grandfather dismissed her reports as the products of a young girl's imagination, inflamed by puberty and aggravated by her genius, but nevertheless had an old acquaintance from the New Orleans Police Department—Desforge *père* worked in the DA's office for a brief stint in his twenties—inspect the house for signs of entry. The policeman assured my mother she was safe; yet she knew otherwise.

A week later she was unable to move her fingers. The intruders, she claimed, were stealing into her room each night to tighten wood clamps on those fingers, just enough to splinter the bones with hairline cracks but not break them completely. And because she couldn't move her fingers, she couldn't paint; she stopped going to her art classes, and her after-school hours, formerly filled with long painting sessions during which my grandparents would leave her dinner outside her bedroom door, turned listless and gray. As day switched to night, she would sit at the foot of her bed and stare at her immobile hands. Soon she began speaking in something like tongues, nonsensical blather that came streaming from her mouth in emotional torrents, like impenetrable lingual salads hurled from a shooter. She decided her father was in cahoots with the intruders, along with her schoolteachers, and she refused to be alone with him in a room or to go to school. At this point my grandparents naturally should have sought medical help but they felt certain this was the dark lining of the silver cloud of genius and would pass, like a cold that broth and bedrest would cure. Then, on a weekday morning in the winter of 1950, she surrendered to the earthly conspiracy against her. She'd give them the absence they wanted. One by one, she emptied all of her oil paints into her mouth, cadmium yellow and lead white and arsenic-laced cobalt blue—a garish, self-annihilating palette squeezed down her throat.

As suicide attempts go, it was a weak one. (She'd get better at it over the years—oh, much fucking better.) My grandmother found her lying on her bedroom floor, rainbows of drool leaking from the corners of her mouth, but Willa vomited up the paint before her stomach had to be pumped. It was, I've sometimes imagined (albeit abstractly), the world's most beautiful vomit: a gastric rendition of Joseph's coat of many colors, its wild variegation and vivid chromatic streaks a pooling rebuke to the black mind that sought to swallow them. Immediately my grandparents, stricken and confused, admitted her to Tulane Hospital, where the first of her nightmare bouts of insulin coma therapy began.

She told me about it, once, back when I was hospitalized for the drinking and the prognosis looked bleak. The white floors and walls of the ICT ward, the beds and bedstands coated in white ceramic, the starched white uniforms of the nurses, the white-coated doctors who wore bowties so patients couldn't grab hold of dangling neckwear. First came the injection, followed by the salivating. So much saliva that the nurses would sop it with sponges. They would cover her with blankets to ease the chills, and restrain her with folded bedsheets when she thrashed or slipped into a grand mal seizure. And then, after a while, everything would go black, and an hour later she would awaken with a gavage tube up her nose and her sheets soiled, with no clue where she was or who she was—all she would know was that she was hungry, brutally hungry, as if all the humanity had been drained from her leaving one base animal urge. When she was released to her parents, after six weeks of this, she'd gained thirty pounds. Her smile seemed hollow but it was a smile nonetheless, and the doctors pronounced her better—not cured, but better. On the ride home from the hospital my grandparents talked about the weather until there was nothing more they could say about it and were visibly relieved to hear my mother agree that it was "nice." "Yes," said my grandmother. "It *is* nice, isn't it? It's nice. It's good that it's nice."

But the weather didn't stay nice and my mother had to be readmitted, for another fifty days of ICT, when she was nineteen. It was three weeks after this second round of treatment that the possum moved into the attic on Tonti Street, and roughly five weeks thereafter that Gerald Desforge, unable to endure further pleading from his daughter, called Dixie Pest Control on Airline Highway and asked that someone please please puhleeze come save the dwindling animal cornered in his attic.

Henryk Gniech was who they sent. A big dumb-looking

Polack with oily corkscrewed hair and thin crinkled eyes and a 36-inch inseam and a 32-inch waist, skinny and mute as a light-pole. His English was barely serviceable. After four years in the U.S., Henryk could understand most of what he heard — except from blacks, who he was convinced spoke a different language altogether — but he found it damnably hard to form the English words in his mouth. The vowels and consonants slaughtered one another on his tongue, fell dead and mushy from his lips. "We got a possum up here that's giving my daughter conniptions," said my grandfather. "I don't know how long these critters can last but this one's not going down easy." Henryk Gniech merely nodded, trailing my grandfather up the stairs. "Between us, I figured the lack of water would've dropped the damn thing in a week or so. Not that I want a dead possum stinking up the house but my daughter has real fragile nerves and that scratching just rips her in two." Henryk nodded again, scanning the hallway ceiling as if studying tea leaves. "Up here's the attic," said my grandfather.

Just then my mother's bedroom door opened. She'd been napping and her eyes were red and pinched and her hair was wild, a volcanic display of black serpents. "Who's this?" she said to her father. Her accusatory tone was by now familiar.

"Man from Dixie Pest Control," he said. "He doesn't speak English. You speak English?"

Henryk nodded, staring at Willa who was staring back.

"He says he speaks English," muttered my grandfather, then said again, much louder and slower than before: "Up here's the attic."

Willa's eyes drifted down to the Ketch-All pole in Henryk's hand, a steel rod with a wire noose at one end. Stepping from the doorway, with a drowsy-drunk half-stumble, she said, "He's not going to kill it."

"He's going to get rid of it," said my grandfather. "Like you wanted."

"He aims to kill it," she said. "That's a lynching tool."

"A lynching tool? Hush, ain't no such thing. That's a possum grabber. Come on up here, Pest Man," he said, putting a hand to Henryk's back and directing him up the attic stairs. "She's brilliant, like I was saying, but has really fine, fine nerves," Willa heard her father say. She stood at the foot of the stairs and hollered up: "I want to see it. I want to see it . . . moving."

After two or three minutes she heard a scuffling from above —quick scratches and the thump of boots on the attic planks, reverbed footfalls she thought she could almost see dimpling the ceiling—and rat-a-tat shouts from her father ("Get er now, over there, *get er*"). From below Willa screamed—a silly scream, I imagine, like that of the housewife exiled onto a footstool in the old Tom & Jerry cartoons. "What is it?" her father yelled down; he'd learned, as I later would, to take nothing for granted, not even a cartoon matron's wimpy shriek. "What's happening?" she shouted back up. "Don't you come up here," said her father, flooding her with dread. "Don't you dare let him kill it," she responded, her voice caught somewhere between a plea and a screamy demand and crackling in that middle ground. "I'll never forgive you or anyone ever again." (Ah, typical Willa Desforges hyperbole. "If you continue to bite your fingernails," she told me when I was a boy, "you will never be loved. No one will want you and you will die alone.")

Henryk Gniech descended first from the attic. Cradled in his arms was the possum, its wet dark eyes flickering back and forth, random as a flame, but its body still, its claws anchored in the sleeves of Henryk's canvas jacket, its small pink tongue limply extended. Henryk's hands—huge hands, Willa noticed, with the elongated fingers of a French Quarter stride pianist —were around it like a loose net. Brandishing the Ketch-All tool, and panting, Gerald Desforge stood behind him on the stairs. "The boy scooped him up like a pro," he said, obviously exhilarated. Willa was overcome by concurrent desires to touch and to recoil from the possum, and its carrier, and for a moment she lost her balance, wobbling toward the wall.

"They ack dead," Henryk said, his first words to her. "Is sweet."

"Where will he take it?" she asked her father. Then, correcting herself, to Henryk: "Where will you take it?"

With a shrug, he said, "A tree."

"Not one around here, though," said Gerald Desforges.

"Far away," said Henryk.

She didn't think he would kill it, not the way he was holding it, but she said anyway, almost as a question, "You're not going to kill it."

"City Park," her father said. "He can take it to the park."

"I'm going with you," she said to Henryk. "I don't trust you." This was a lie. She did trust him. Though a hired killer, he had the eyes of an old priest, of a dispenser of daily mercies rather than acrid poison. With fierce and prolonged harrumphs, her father objected—but of course he relented, he always did. He'd go to his deathbed fearing entanglement in her nerves.

Willa waited in the Dixie Pest Control truck—spartan and filthy, the floorboards swamped with empty Coke bottles—while Henryk locked the possum in a rusty steel cage in the truckbed. The Coke bottles clinked together as he drove through New Orleans, filling the otherwise silent cab with a glassy random music.

"You must usually kill them," she said after a while.

"No," he said. The bottles chinkled in a pothole crescendo. "I have . . . secret place. I give gift."

"Where?"

"Is beautiful. Most beautiful place. I show you. You want I show you?"

As he piloted the truck through New Orleans she tried to

guess where he would stop, wondering what beauty might look like to a Polish exterminator, but—down Claiborne Street, then onto Rampart and then St. Claude and into the Bywater —the possibilities kept dwindling. A *gift*, he'd said. With a prick of horror she wondered if he intended to deliver the possum to a down-and-out black family in the Lower Ninth Ward, to cook and eat. Fear of fricassee roiled her insides. But then he turned onto Poland Avenue and kept driving toward the river until there was no more road to drive upon, and he stopped the truck at the wharf. He was grinning as he shut off the motor, as if everything—the beauty, the possum's fate—was gorgeously self-evident.

"I'm confused," she said, and something in her expression— distaste, disappointment—broke his smile. Together, in separate silences, they surveyed the scene: the Mississippi River, so muddy and drab that it barely reflected sunlight; the drydocks across the river in Algiers; the freighters and banana boats with rust stains leaking down their hulls like blood from wounds; old squat warehouses, tin-roofed terminal offices, decomposing boxcars, dry plains of concrete. She inhaled the odors of fishguts, sulfur, and shipsmoke. *Is beautiful*, he'd said. Finally, she might have thought (though she's rarely been prone to self-deprecation): Someone crazier than me.

"Most beautiful place," he said, his tone adding half a question mark to the statement. Gently, she shook her head no: my parents' first disagreement.

This is how he explained it (with tender enthusiasm, but brokenly, asking her constantly to fill the gaps in his story with the words he didn't know): Four years earlier, a ship from Germany had docked at the Poland Avenue Wharf, a fitting place of disembarkation for the ninety-three Polish refugees who came squinting down its gangplank. Most of them were Jews, and most survivors of the Nazi concentration camps, their inner forearms blued with their camp tattoos. A brass band was there to greet them, along with throngs of volunteers from the Red Cross and the United Service for New Americans, their biceps striped in colorful armbands. Among the arrivals was Henryk Gniech.

I do not know (with certainty, anyway) which labor camp my father survived, or what happened to him there. (Dachau, we believe—that's where the priests ended up.) We know he was a Catholic seminary student who was arrested for wearing a cassock. He told my mother this much. (For several years a member of the Catholic Patron League of New Orleans, which had sponsored his immigration, would visit to gauge his religious temperature; they'd expected him to resume his seminary studies and become a priest, something he'd never intended to do. They stopped coming after my mother entered the picture.) We know, too, that all his family died in the war, and that, along with whatever else he suffered, he was whipped terribly; his back bore a rubbery pink lattice of scars. He never spoke of any of it except, my mother suspected, in his sleep, when he would sometimes sob and utter what sounded to my mother (who never learned Polish) like dark pleas. "Like a child trapped down in a well," my mother put it. No, in rewinding his life, my father never went beyond this one sunlit point: stepping onto the hot concrete of New Orleans, the docks swarming with the soft welcoming chaos of charity workers, the moist air filled with the garish and inappropriate tuba-honks of "When the Saints Go Marching In," which would forever remain his favorite song. (He hummed it as he shaved, showered, scanned the *Times-Picayune*, munched peanuts on the couch.) He considered this his birth, the beginning of Him, as if everything that had come before comprised a lightless womb from which he'd squeezed free.

So this was where Henryk Gniech freed the possum, as he'd freed an ark's worth of pestilent creatures before. The possum sniffed at the air, took several meek steps from the cage, then skittered across the concrete into a safe crevice between two giant wooden crates, disappearing from sight. This was my father's gift—a second chance on the docks—the greatest gift he knew—the same one he'd himself been given. He smiled, lit a cigarette, hummed the opening bars of "When the Saints . . . ," and returned the empty cage to the truck while Willa stood there staring, watching that dark merciful crevice with the same rapt and emotional attention she might give a Degas in the museum. She had not expected this, no. A new kind of madness. She fell in love that afternoon, and within three weeks she was pregnant.

————

WELL, SHIT. That was a much longer interlude than I'd intended. Are you still there? I am. Still here, I mean. I had to relocate midway through that sepia burst of genealogy because some twiddledee with an acoustic guitar decided to serenade the masses assembled at Gate K9 with an instrumental rendition of "Dust in the Wind." This wouldn't have been so toxic —all we are, after all, is dust in the wind—had he not kept flubbing the changes and, rather than pushing forward with the song, repeating them until he got them right. First time I can recall that I've ever heard a guitar *stutter*. (Revision, like any other grooming procedure, should be kept private.—The Book of B. Ford, 2:13.) I'm now at Gate K12 which seems safe except for this young skinnymarink Asian fellow across from me who keeps chuckling at some apparently textual dialogue he's having with his cellphone. Back in my undergrad days, when the pocket calculator made its first appearance, I kept myself very mildly entertained in math classes by making words out of the squared numerals: 800 for BOO, for example. 5318008, upside down, for BOOBIES. 58008618, likewise, for BIGBOOBS. Ah, what hilarity! I don't suppose that's what my young Asiatic friend is doing though the physical motions are rather precisely reminiscent. It occurs to me just now that if they were to make a mega-sized cellphone—with buttons the size of, say, Lucky Strike packs—my mother could send me text messages instead of so laboriously writing me her shaky-scrawl Post-it notes. Of course, I'd need to be equipped with a cellphone myself for that to work. But still: What a triumph of technology that would be—her Post-it notes finding me any-where, out on the streets or inside a crosstown bus, pinned to the wings of digital homing pigeons.

As to Miss Willa, and the above: These are the facts as I know them, but since the source for them is my mother, pass the salt. Though there's a certain logic to the story. How else could a rawboned & half-mute Polish refugee/extermina-tor have seduced my mother? Frankly if he hadn't been such a gentle man I might speculate I was born of rape. But then of course, dear American Airlines, you don't give a possum's pink ass as to how or why I was conceived. At this point you're doubtless wishing that I'd never *been* conceived, and I'd be ly-ing if I denied being on your side on that one. Add Stella to the bleachers and we could all do a wave. Anyway, I apologize for that sideways waltz into the story of my beginnings. It's clear I should've been a Russian novelist: I can't even write a fucking refund request without detailing my lineage.

Not that this is any fucking refund request, mind you. I'm not sure it's clear just yet but there was a lot more than $392.68 riding on this flight.

- - - -

MAYBE I SHOULD EXPLAIN.

In the winter of 1978 I became a new father. This wasn't, I should note, by design: As I was an accident of conception, so too was my daughter. An accident begat an accident. In our case, it was a night spent atop a patchwork of blankets on a sec-ond-story porch that led to the startlement of unexpected parenthood. I'd just moved in with Stella after a delirious three-month courtship, lugging mostly books—in fact, I don't think I contributed anything *but* books—into her upstairs apartment in a double gallery house in the Irish Channel. A typical grad-student rental place, slummy and peeling but charming in that bohemian way. Since this was the first night in our home we celebrated by cooking something oystery out of my dead grandmother's copy of the *Picayune's Creole Cookbook* and opening a jug of Gallo Rhine wine which at the time we thought was something special. It was a warm spring night, the blooming magnolias infusing the whole Channel with a lemonade smell, so we moved outside to the gallery. Stella lit candles and we smoked a joint and told stories that made us both laugh beyond the brink of tears and, at some point, while we were making love—and however distasteful I find that euphemism, that's precisely what we were doing—with her atop me, I spelled out I LOVE YOU with a fingertip on the wet skin of her back. We stayed out there all night, circled at dawn by bright puddles of melted candlewax.

In those months we were the planet's happiest residents. If I was no longer the *poète maudit*, well, *pbbbbbt*, I didn't give a damn. I stopped drinking alone and suicide was as improbable a concept for me as joining a Kiwanis Club. On the hi-fi, the morose West Coast blues pianists I specialized in listening to were replaced by mindless rock. For silly kicks we put ABBA on the turntable. I wrote nothing but reveled in my giddy muteness. I chopped vegetables and paid bills. I delivered hot tea to Stella when she was studying and read aloud to her while she soaked in our rust-stained tub. The salad days, they're called, though I've no clue why.

It took her a while to tell me she was pregnant. Stella claims she wanted to wring as much happiness out of the unclouded present as she could—and that if perhaps she didn't say it aloud, didn't grant it that oral credence, it might pass like a fever. That conversation, when it finally came, was pocked with terrible long silences. I told her it was up to her, what to do, though I was hoping she'd abort the pregnancy. We were young, rootless, intent on scouring the ends of the earth. And I doubted—correctly, as it turned out—my potential as a father. The next day she made an appointment at a clinic in Gentilly and for the next two weeks we drifted in slow awful orbit around the unspoken. I had nightmares I didn't reveal to her; or rather, not nightmares, but oblique dreams about losing things. One in which Charles's prized guitar was stolen from my car, another about my share of the rent money disappearing from my desk drawer. On the couch one night we watched a movie, a late-night replaying of *Brian's Song*, and at the end, when James Caan's character died, I noticed she was crying—sobbing. I put my arms around her and said, "I forgot how sad the ending to this movie was," and she replied, quickly, "I'm not crying because James Caan is dead." Just as quickly I said, "I know," but that was a lie. For all I knew she could have been mourning James Caan; the truth was, I didn't know what she was feeling. When we went to bed that night I lay there holding her in my arms, spooning, until the typical sprouting of a hard-on prompted me to shimmy backwards beneath the sheets, to skitter as far away as I could get from her. I didn't want her to feel it. *She'll realize it was me*, I thought dumbly. *Me that did it to her, me that's making her cry.*

She didn't ask me to go with her but I did. The clinic occupied a house on a residential street, with only a vague insignia on the exterior—some archetypal female figure, in a robe, raising her hands to the sky—to distinguish it from its neighbors. There was a guard outside, too, a fat chainsmoking black guy who avoided eye contact. Inside, a waiting room evoked a struggling inner-city dental office, with magazines enfolded in those SUBSCRIPTION EXPIRING! THIS IS YOUR LAST ISSUE! wrappers and Gordon Lightfoot's "Rainy Day People" being piped from ceiling speakers. I held her hand until her name was called. I hadn't brought anything to read, as that seemed inappropriate, so mostly I stayed outside and smoked cigarettes, uncomfortably sharing an ashtray with the guard. But I had time for only one or two cigarettes, because within fifteen minutes Stella appeared on the porch. Her cheeks were red and blistered with tears and she was clutching her thin sweatercoat to her as if stricken with a paralyzing chill. "I'm sorry," she said. "I can't go through with it. Bennie, I'm sorry but I can't." I moved to embrace her but she stepped back. "No," she said. "No, let's go. Let's please please get out of here."

The best that I can say about the next eight months is that we tried. We cleared out the second bedroom, which had just been transformed into my writing room, and installed a crib and a changing table. We bought *Goodnight Moon* and *Bedtime for Frances* at the Maple Street Book Shop and, from a French Quarter shop, some souvenir voodoo dolls we thought would be kooky/funny to stock in the crib. Because we needed money, I jumped to the other side of the bar at the Exchange, switching from barfly to bartender; Felix the Fat even put a plastic jar with a sign that read BENNIE'S BABY FUND on the bar, though that disappeared as soon as Stella heard about it. At night I put my ear to her belly and tried to listen and feel but always there was nothing. "You don't *feel* that?" she would say. "There. That one. That was a kick." I didn't. Often I was aimlessly angry and sometimes I was thrilled but mostly I was terrified. One night, after closing the bar, I drank myself unconscious, and the next morning Felix called an ambulance because he couldn't rouse me from the floor. He later told me he even tried kicking me in the nuts. As you'd expect, Stella wasn't pleased. A few nights later the sounds of something shattering woke me around three A.M. Stella's side of the bed was empty so I called out her name. More crashes & shatters. I ran to the kitchen and found her standing over the sink, sobbing while throwing our dishes and glasses in one at a time. Shards were everywhere. I held her and let her cry and then led her back to bed before cleaning up the sharp mess. We never spoke of it again despite the conspicuous barrenness of our cupboards.

Stella Clarinda Ford was born in January: The name Stella was for her mother, of course, and Clarinda we cribbed from Robert Burns ("Fair Empress of the Poet's Soul, and Queen of Poetesses . . ."). It occurs to me that I should also clarify the surname, i.e. Ford and not Gniech. That was my father's doing in the months before I was born. Miss Willa, bound by propriety to marry the Polish exterminator who'd impregnated her, nonetheless refused to become Willa Gniech. ("A Willa Gniech sounds like a troll from Norse mythology," she told Henryk. "Or an epic sneeze.") So without consulting her he went down to the courthouse and changed his name to the most American one he could conjure: Henry Ford. (His ignorance of his chosen namesake's anti-Semitism, considering what he'd been through during the war, added another layer of ridiculousness to it. Yet he was devoutly loyal ever after to Ford vehicles and when he later became a mechanic he would joke that he preferred working on Fords because it was a "family bizz-a-ness.") There was loose talk between Stella and me, prior to Stella Jr.'s birth, about dropping the Ford surname for the authentic Gniech, partly to horrify my mother, but Stella Sr. couldn't help agreeing about the epic sneeze. ("Or an obscene Russian drinking toast," she added. "*Stella Gniech!*")

When I held my daughter in my arms for the first time, naturally I broke down crying. She was so beautiful and small—a gorgeous pink speck of life. But I should also confess that I was drunk almost beyond recognition. I was working when Stella's water broke but she said it was okay, her mother was there, and since the labor would no doubt be long I could join her as soon as my shift was over. But the labor wasn't long and not two hours later her mother called the bar to announce the birth. Of course everybody bought me shots and there was a grand brou-haha with many more rounds of congratulatory shots and, as sometimes happens when you're drinking, time slipped away. All the regulars stayed past closing and Felix locked the doors and brought out some champagne, and Crazy Jane, slapping the bar, called for cognac which she pronounced "COG-nack." When I finally got to the hospital I was so brazenly sloshed that a policeman tried to stop me from entering but I said my new baby daughter was in there so he accompanied me up to the maternity ward. He was standing right beside me when I lifted Stella Jr. from the hospital crib, tears dribbling from my eyes, along with a nurse who hovered nearby with her hands splayed out to catch the baby if I dropped her. "Go home, Bennie," Stella's mother told me. A London-born professor of British lit at Pepperdine, she had this crisp way of speaking that made her every utterance sound like an arch dismissal; when she was truly dismissing you, it struck like lightning. "For God's sake take yourself home." Stella was asleep the whole time and I lightly kissed her forehead before the policeman escorted me outside. As I staggered off into the dark he advised me to put some sausage-biscuits in my belly, adding a shout of congratu-lations when I was almost too far away to hear.

DEAR AMERICAN AIRLINES, enclosed please find my sciatic nerve. Due to the wear and tear on it from hours upon hours in this miserable fucking O'Hare seating—these patent-pending O'Chairs—I am sending it to you for speedy repair. A return envelope is also enclosed, which you may address to me care of the wheelchair bank across from Gate K8, Chicago, Ill.

I'm not kidding about the wheelchairs. In fact, I'm planted in one right now. They're unattended and apparently free-range and since I saw some young buck lounging in another one, I figured what the hell. Obviously I promise to jump out at the first sight of a struggling cripple. They're actually the most comfortable spots in the airport save for the "Sleep Number" bed on display in the alleyway between the K and H concourses, which the young buck informs me is currently under siege. "Some dude offered the salesguy, like, two hundred bucks to let him sleep on it tonight," he told me. "Then some other dude anted up five hundred. There's, like, no hotel rooms in the whole freakin' city. They're totally gonna be fighting over that bed by midnight. God, that'd be awesome. The salesguy looks freaked." I suggested that I might wheel myself over there and try to con some Samaritans into lifting me onto the bed, and then wait to see who'd actually try to evict a napping cripple. The kid loved this idea. "Dude," he said respectfully, "you're sick."

I realize that the preceding explained almost nothing about my current predicament—nix that; *our* current predicament —and for that I apologize. "I'm getting there," as I sometimes tell editors inquiring about the pace of my translations. And I hope I'm not laying too much on you but for the first time in my life I'm trying to be honest, trying to set the record straight. You must understand that, at this point, running my life through the spin cycle isn't liable to do me any good. Self-mythologizing, like drinking for fourteen hours a day, will eventually grind you into residue. You look in the mirror one morning and realize: That face, this life, these weren't my intention. Who's that baggy-eyed motherfucker and how'd he get into my mirror? That said, I would've no doubt saved us both a lot of grief had I just claimed up front to be on my way to L.A. to donate my left kidney to a bedridden orphan named Tiny something-or-other. We could have bidden each other hello and farewell in the space of a single heartwarming page. Yeah, well. Yet another opportunity that I've pissed away with words.

From my vantage in this wheelchair I can see the sunset

through the windows. It's a brilliant, operatic one, flame-colored, with the planes cooking on the tarmac luminescent with orange glints. A postcard of hell as seen from purgatory. Or heaven, it's so hard to tell from here.

- - - -

BUT LET'S RETURN TO '79. I'll shoot for brevity, but as should be clear it's not my strong suit.

My Stella was never the reckless sort—a birth-control pill snafu, rather than unguarded passion, had brought us to the present—but I was nonetheless surprised, once we were all home, by the degree of her protectiveness with Stella Jr., whom I called "Speck." Stella claimed I held her wrong, scolded me for tickling her because I might "upset her organs," asked me not to change her diapers anymore because I wasn't thorough enough with the wiping and sometimes forgot to dash her bottom with powder. Once I tried dancing with Speck—a clumsy little father-daughter two-step through the living room—and Stella leapt off the couch as if I'd been winding up my arm to toss Speck out the window. "You're going to *hurt* her," she said, stealing her away with an ironic roughness. She'd get the baby to sleep every night in the crib but after a few hours Speck would cry and Stella would carry her to our bed. At this point I would have to leave because Stella was worried I'd roll over and smother the baby, so after a few weeks I gave up trying and started making myself a bed on the couch on my nights off from the bar. It was lonely out in the living room, so I reverted to old habits by mixing consolatory batches of vodka-tonics. Because I knew Stella would be disturbed by the sight of empty Smirnoff fifths, I hid my empties behind the books in the bookcase and sneaked them out *en masse* when the Stellas were out walking or "making groceries" as we said in New Orleans.

As to those groceries: Stella's parents were helping us financially and my own mother was intermittently generous (she thought it was poor taste to give money so she peppered the nursery with Steiff teddy bears and pewter rattles from Maison Blanche; all this while our television sat atop salvaged cinder blocks and we shared a single water glass). But money was still tight, so I picked up an extra shift at the Exchange after Bobby, who worked the choice Friday and Ladies' Night shifts, got pissed at Felix in the wee hours and knocked him to the floor with a fifth of Cluny Scotch.

Which brings me to my own issue with violence at the bar. Some lawyers came in one evening—the neighborhood was changing, its fixer-upper houses and vegetarian, drum-circle vibe attracting what would later come to be called yuppies— and were sitting at the corner by the door getting rip-roaring drunk on gin martinis, which were then and there so unfashionable that I actually had to look up how to make one. Bona fide asshole types—the kind of guys still wearing their college ring at forty and telling you what channel they "need" the TV over the bar to be on. One of them was talking about a paralegal he'd recently "knocked up" and chortling about it, which elicited a caustic brag from another that he'd been to the abortion clinic so many times they'd given him a "Buy Ten, Get the Next One Free" card.

I'd been drinking pretty hard—standard protocol behind the bar at the Exchange—and, to boot, a day earlier I'd had a rough row with Charles who'd called me a "washout" who should "stick to breeding" since that's where my true talents seemed to lie. All of which, I'm sure, colored my subsequent actions.

I mixed the Buy-Ten-Get-One-Free guy what's known in the trade as a "cement mixer": a jigger of Bailey's Irish Cream paired with a jigger of lime juice. This combination produces a curdling-type reaction in the mouth, instantly transforming the liquids into a cheesy, semisolid wad. It's a folkloric cocktail for wreaking vengeance, not for drinking. Because they were all wearing swell neckties I even carefully layered it like a *pousse café*.

"Compliments of the house, and appreciate y'all stopping in," I said, sliding it in front of Buy-Ten then turning my back to him. I heard Buy-Ten say thanks and imagined him puffing up ever so slightly: *Dig this, boys, I'm a hero of the loafing class.* B. B. Mike was sitting down near that end of the bar and had witnessed the making of the drink with the quizzical, head-cocked look of a bewildered but ugly puppy. From his expression alone, as he watched Buy-Ten throw it back, I rightly determined the impact of my cement mixer, but the sound effects were equally suggestive: a gurgling-gargling, a gasping for air, followed by a resounding and spitty *What the fuck?!?* When I turned around, Buy-Ten's tongue was hanging limply from his mouth and his tie was marbled with cum-like streaks of curdled Irish liqueur. I could probably have weaseled my way out of the situation at that point—truth be told, I was feeling almost sorry for the guy—had B. B. Mike, a short, stout cigar-chomper who was a dead ringer for Paulie in the *Rocky* movies, not launched into the largest, longest laugh of his life. His cap tipped backwards off his head and I believe he even held his chest with one hand while pointing with the other. I had no idea that shrieks such as those could emanate from a man such as that. Nor had I any idea that a trio of Uptown lawyers would scramble over a bar to kick the living shit out of an errant bartender. (At the time, I suppose I thought they took priest-like vows.)

They pulped me pretty grimly—I had to get stitches in two places and both my eyes were blackened—but the rest of the bar's occupants, excepting B. B. Mike who was winded from laughing so hard, mounted a riotous counteroffensive that resulted in one of the lawyers (the paralegal-knocker-upper) getting his jaw broken and face lacerated by—you guessed it—a fifth of Cluny's. (Felix the Fat never served Cluny's again, calling it "cursed.") It was an unusual barfight in that it took place almost entirely *behind* the bar, the spatial equivalent of a heavyweight boxing title being fought in a shower stall, which also meant there was lots of damage. Dead Fred's urn got knocked from its sacred upper shelf and his ashes were strewn everywhere. I heard later that Felix made the sign of the cross nonstop while hosing Dead Fred off the floor mats.

I got suspended for two weeks but that wasn't nearly the worst of it. The *Times-Picayune* got wind of the brawl and an overambitious reporter framed it as a repercussion of the neighborhood's tensions—the junkies/hippies/freaks rising up against the suited gentrifiers. The reporter even referenced Hunter S. Thompson's old Freak Power campaign in Aspen and made ironic hay about the bar being named the Turf Exchange. It would have been nice to be a folk hero but the story also noted that the cause of the initial fight was "a conflict over a woman," a not entirely incorrect misconception that must (I've always presumed) have stemmed from B. B. Mike who'd been eavesdropping on the lawyers like me. Probably he said, in classical Mike-speak, that the lawyers had been "talking shit about some broad," and that was enough for the reporter who, ambition notwithstanding, never gave me the courtesy of a call.

Imagine Stella's reaction. Then square it, and square it again, then multiply it by crazy. She'd been suspicious when I came home from the emergency room, all stitched-up and black-eyed, because I couldn't really explain the cause of the quarrel. "Babe, they were jackass *lawyers*," I said, as if that resolved everything. But she knew my conciliatory, hippie-poet ways—not to mention the high tolerance I had, owing to my grandfather, for New Orleans lawyers—well enough to sense missing pieces. But what could I say? We'd never talked about what happened at the clinic—she flatly refused—and there seemed no exculpatory defense, in her eyes, for my reaction to

Buy-Ten's smarmy boast. "What?" I imagined her screaming. "Were you *envious?*" Or perhaps taking the opposite position and accusing me of secretly hating her because she'd chosen, on her own, to abort Speck—nevermind that she didn't follow through with it, and that I was the one who drove her to Gentilly. (By this time I'd been theorizing that her taut overprotectiveness with Stella Jr. might derive from that turnabout.) Frankly I didn't want to reintroduce the word "abortion" into our vocabulary; the psychic wounds still oozed. And what's worse: I *couldn't* honestly explain what had happened—why I'd poured that cement mixer—because to do that would expose the great black hole that I was feeling in my life, the loneliness and constriction and sense of dreams irredeemably deferred, the dankness I felt mixing myself my seventh vodka-tonic on the couch at night, and I didn't see how I could confess all this to Stella without her concluding that I didn't love Speck, her, or the both of them. So I stonewalled.

I kept stonewalling even after the paper arrived two mornings later, which in retrospect was resoundingly stupid. As the old saw counsels: If you're trapped in a hole, stop digging. That morning we had a terrible fight made even more terrible by Speck's relentless bawling. When Stella demanded to know who the "whore" was, I broke into mirthless but uproarious laughter because the word "whore" was so ludicrous and un-Stella-like. The laughter enraged her enough that she ordered me to move out and, to help me start the process, in a frenzy she swept shelves' worth of my books off the bookcase, letting them crash to the floor. Of course it didn't help that a half-dozen empty Smirnoff bottles rolled after them. Clink, clink. Clinkclinkclink.

Overwhelmed, she collapsed to the floor in a puddle of sobs and let me hold her there for a time and even let me fetch her a glass of water which I thought spelled progress. Very calmly she asked again who the "whore" was, and this time I didn't laugh but told her, with proper gravitas, that there was no whore and never had been. "Oh, Bennie," she said, wagging her head. "Bennie, Bennie, goddamnit Bennie." She studied the water glass for a long silent while, sitting amidst the empty fifths and the splayed books, before smashing it into my face. Yep: surprised me too. Blood and glass exploded everywhere and I was instantly blind in one of my blackened eyes. Dumbfounded, all I could say was "You know that was our only glass." I held a reddening t-shirt to my face while Stella drove me to the hospital with poor Speck wailing in the carseat. When they asked me what had happened, in the emergency room, I proclaimed myself a "revolutionary" and said the nurses needed only to check the day's *Picayune* for proof. That brought the attention of the cop on duty whom I satisfied with a story about colliding with a water glass in my wife's hand when I bent down to pick up the (fictional) cat. "Must be *some* pussy," he said, whether referring to the wife or the cat I wasn't sure.

We lasted another eight months, some of them better than others. Because we were low on cash, Stella removed my stitches rather than paying a doctor to do it. It was a weirdly placid night, almost beautiful in its way, or rather *belle laide* as the French would say: beautiful-ugly. I sat in a ladderback chair beneath the gothic chandelier in our living room, lightly sipping a vodka-tonic, as she pulled out the stitches with tweezers while Speck rolled on the floor giggling and saying *dur-dur-dur.* Maybe it was the vodka but that night as we made love for the first time in weeks I found myself weeping and unable to stop. I was crying so badly that we had to pause midway through. With her head against my rising, falling chest Stella asked, softly, if I was crying from joy or sadness and I responded, "Both." There in the dark she sponged away my tears with her lips. We finished with gorged screams, more than a rarity for us, and Stella fell into a contented-looking sleep, a quarter-smile on her face. Since childbirth she'd developed a snore

42

—a gentle chordal exhale, like someone sighing through the low holes of a harmonica—and that night I lay awake listening to the music of her breathing and wondering what the hell love was and if this was it. After a while I gingerly lifted her arm off me and made myself a vodka-tonic which I drank sitting on the edge of the bed, watching her sleep. There was no moon but the streetlamp outside the bedroom window cast a white glow upon her that seemed nothing short of sacred. In these moments it was easy to believe that she loved me and I loved her and that everything was as it should be, in an alternate galaxy for which that streetlamp was the sun.

Yet such nights were uncommon and perhaps it's unduly sentimental to dwell upon them. Near the end I was trying to write again and it wasn't going well. Post-Speck, Stella had abandoned poetry and I felt I was expected to do the same. "You're a *father*," she said, as if drawing an impenetrable line between poet and parent. "So was William Carlos Williams," I said. "You're not Williams," came her accurate if deflating rejoinder. Charles and I patched things up and I took to drinking with him on my nights off, first occasionally and then regularly. Charles cultivated a posse of art-minded coeds and there always seemed to be some fresh and earthily alluring girl with an apparent Eeyore fetish telling me I looked "sad," brushing the hair out of my eyes until I'd swat her hand away. One night, in the alley beside the Exchange where I'd led a member of Charles's coterie longing to share a joint, I found myself kissing a twenty-one-year-old from a place called Hot Coffee, Mississippi, whose humid accent was like sorghum to my addled mind. This brief interlude might have tipped further had she not whispered, "I'll do the things she won't." I'm not sure why I was so offended but when Charles tried to stop me from storming out of the bar I pushed his arm away and told him to stay the fuck away from me blah blah fuck you blah. Once at home I lay on the couch, as always, and drank myself to sleep in front of the salt-colored static on the TV. Maybe I even talked to the static, blah blah fuck you blah, I don't know. That night I hated everyone, particularly myself. This feeling only deepened the next morning when I awoke to the sight of Stella sitting a foot away from me atop the coffee table, crying. It was a mellow, defeated cry. "Look at you," she said to me. I didn't protest, or ask what to look for. Frankly I didn't even try to look.

When the end finally came, we were having—to my mind —another one of those frail good nights. Stella cooked her famous spaghetti & meatballs ("If I shut my eyes almost but not quite all the way, when you're cooking this," I used to tell her, "I see you as an old fat Italian mama with a dark mustache"; she hated this though I meant it with vast affection), and *Fantasy Island* was on the TV set. Stella's adorably snobbish contempt for TV popped like a soap bubble after Speck was born. Sometimes I'd find her and the baby curled on the couch, watching gameshows—hypnotized by Wink Martindale. The downstairs neighbors were out of town so I entertained Speck with some cloddish tapdancing on the old wood floor and even Stella—I think—was laughing. Or maybe I just imagined she was laughing—desire painting perception. In any case, this was the scene: the three of us on the couch, awash in the television's bluesy glow though mostly ignoring *Fantasy Island* because it turned out to be a repeat, Stella and me trading our child back and forth, rubbing our noses against hers, tickling her lips to make her grin. To me the evening looked and felt like peace—not domestic détente, but the real thing. A field of lavender, a northern lake at dawn. Or whatever air-freshener imagery best evokes peace.

Cradling Speck, I said some nonsensical things to her, or rather partly sensical: some sugary riffs about her future. "One day you'll be big, and wear dresses," things like that. I wasn't really paying attention to what I was saying—it was sweet-talk, lulling blather—until I said, "And one day I'm going to walk you down the aisle and hate every second of it," which caused Stella to abruptly stiffen. "Jesus," she murmured.

I sat there bemused. "What?"

She looked away, pursed her lips, then stood up and walked to the door to the gallery. Finally she called me an asshole.

"Because I said I'd hate every second of it? It was a joke. Just a . . . dumb daddy joke."

She was clenching her eyes shut with the heel of her palm pressed against her forehead. "Stella," I said.

"Because you're *lying* to her," she said finally. She peered up at the ceiling and I could see that she'd been clenching her eyes to stanch the flow of tears. Now they ran loose. "I can take you lying to me but hearing you lie to her . . . Jesus, Bennie, we're not doing this anymore." "We" meant the Stellas. "We can't take you anymore."

Back up, I told her. Whoa. We were having a good night. "No," she said. "*You* were having a good night. There are no fucking good nights for us. There's just us wondering if you're coming home and wondering why we should give a damn. *If* we give a damn." I told her that her saying "us" was a little over the top, that dragging Speck into it was unfai—

"Fuck you! Do you hear me? *Fuck* you!" Screaming, pointing, rage as violent and unexpected as lightning shot down from a cloudless blue sky. "Do you have any fucking idea what you've done to me? You were just a goddamned summer fling, a way to pass the time, and now"—slapping her chest—"look. what. the. fuck. you've done to me."

"Because you got pregnant? Is that what this is about?"

A groaning sound. "You don't *get* it. You piece of shit, you don't get it. This has nothing to do with me getting pregnant and nothing to do with her—"

You just said it *was* about her.

"It's about you, Bennie. You don't care about us—not as

people, anyway, not as your daughter and your daughter's mother, not as human beings, as *flesh*."

That's—

"No, *listen*. All you care about, and barely, is the *idea* of us and the *idea* of you sticking by us—you're here in this room right now because you're loyal to the *idea* of Bennie fucking Ford acting like a man and taking care of his family—no, actually I think it's something worse, sometimes I think we're your excuse for failure—but not because you *want* to be here, not because it matters to you that we're here together. We're just more of your props, Bennie. Just like your Lucky Strikes and your stupid loud Underwood typewriter and that stupid tweed cap that makes you look like an out-of-work caddie. We're all of us, cigarettes and child, just movable props in The Life of Benjamin Ford, little figments of your ego."

—

"Jesus, okay, fine. Let's call it your anti-ego. Every day you wake up and try to, to hew to some delusional idea, the same way your mother does though at least she's got a doctor's note, and by the middle of the day, when life isn't aligning with the idea, you start drinking. Why? Because drinking pushes the life and the idea of it closer together, makes them both so foggy that you can't tell them apart. So you keep drinking until, until they're one and the same but by that time it's all fog, and by that time nothing exists outside of your head at all. And then it's *all* idea, and no life. Have you ever even *thought* how the fuck that makes us feel? No. No. Because we're just employees of, of your imagination, and every day, Bennie, every day"—voice cracking—"we feel that imagination turning more and more away from us, or against us."

—

"That's bullshit. My god, you and your *bullshit*. You couldn't even make it to her *birth*. And do you know why? Because the, the actuality of it didn't matter. It didn't matter to you! It was already complete in your head, it was finished. You were a father! *You!* It was all about you, your idea of you, the you preening inside your head, the *word* of it—*father.* So what did it matter that me and my mother and your new daughter were at the hospital? Do you have any fucking clue how that *humiliated* me? A cop dragging you off the elevator to see your child? The nurse asked me, asked me the next morning if I wanted to talk to a *counselor.* She wasn't even on duty when you came in —she'd heard about it from the other nurses. With my mother sitting there, twirling her goddamn pearls, she asked me if I needed a *counselor.* That was supposed to be the happiest day of my life and I spent it vomiting *because of you*, not looking my mother in the eye *because of you*—"

—

"Bennie, life is *real.* It's hard and it hurts and it's nothing like the world in our heads and at some point everyone grows up and realizes that and it doesn't mean they've given up or sold out or died inside, it just means they've learned that the ideas are just that, they're smoke rings, vapor, and that people have to live in the world as it is—"

—

"Give her to me. How dare you. Give her to me now."

—

"Coming from you that's meaningless. Maybe you love yourself loving me but I don't think you could feel the distinction —I don't think you're *capable* of feeling it—"

—

"Yes. Maybe. Maybe I did love you, for a time. But does it even matter anymore, Bennie? I mean, so what? And did it ever really matter to you if I did? Did it? How could it have?"

—

"We want you out of our lives. I don't know what else to say."

—

"Look at her. She's screaming. Do you see what you're *doing* to her? Get away from us, Bennie. Get away. I swear to Christ I'll kill you—"

—

Oh fuck this fuck this fuck this. What am I doing? Some twit wearing camper shorts and a WORLDWIDE MINISTRIES, INC. t-shirt just knelt beside my wheelchair and asked gently if I was okay. No, I take that back, he wasn't a twit. *Enough*, goodbye.

– – – –

ON A BENCH BY THE SEA Walenty lifted his left pantleg above his hinged knee and stared at the false limb, running his hand along its length the way a runner might massage away a cramp. The wood—English willow, the weeping tree— was lacquered, but already the lacquer had worn off in spots and it might be possible to get a splinter; he would have to re-lacquer it every so often, he thought, would have to repaint himself as a steam engine gets refinished, an oddly unnatural task. When the shell had hit he'd been scurrying uphill toward the jagged ruins of a stone house where several Nazi infantrymen were making an ill-considered stand. The Nazis were surrounded and the outcome was inevitable. There was no mystery to the ending, no suspense in the proceedings; all of them, the Nazis and Walenty's regiment and the British troops flanking the north side, were numbers and symbols in an algebraic problem that had already been solved.

When the shell hit, it threw him backwards down the hill. He felt his arm break on the loose remnants of a rock wall —even the muffled crack of the bone splitting registered —and when finally he was still he reached first for his arm, hoping to adjust it to somehow lessen the pain. It seemed like several minutes before he realized his leg was gone.

There was no pain, only a sharp dullness like that of frost-bite. Below his thigh the flesh resembled the dangling ten-tacles of a squid. His vision kept reddening which puzzled him until he brought a hand to his eyes and realized that it was blood, leaking from his head. Even his ears were fill-ing with it. He lay back on the stones and let the blood flow out of him. He thought he should pray but couldn't bring himself to make the words. Instead he thought of the *mako-wiec* his mother used to make for dessert on rare special days when he was a boy. Expecting the end, he consoled himself with visions of poppyseed cake. Later, in the field hospital, his mind creamy with morphine, Walenty had been unsure what disturbed him more: his lost limb and the shrapnel holes in his forehead, or that the only crumbs of life that he found to cling to, when dying on the battlefield, were cake crumbs.

It's nighttime now, and after a couple of trembly but fortify-ing cigarettes outside, and yet another joyous pat-down at the security checkpoint, I've moved to the bar at the Chili's Too across from G9. I had to wait in a line ten-deep for a barstool, and I can feel the hot stares from those still waiting, like poison darts thwacking my backside. Ouch! I suppose it *is* the height of rudeness to occupy this valuable stool with no set purpose in mind, other than blasting off page after page of this intermina-ble letter while sipping $1.75 club sodas (no ice) and occasion-ally checking in on Walenty—all this while my fellow refu-gees stand in puckered silence, transferring their carry-on bags from one achy shoulder to the other, wanting only a cold Mi-chelob and the televised box scores. It crosses my mind to buy them all a beer but they're mostly devoid of free hands plus there's probably a Homeland Security rule against that. Sorry, chumps. No beer Samaritan for you.

I see from the television hanging in the corner that the price of oil is skyrocketing and that the NASDAQ was down for the day. Poor NASDAQ. I may send it a get-well card—something cheery, of course, like a Snoopy card. But horrors! The British pound sterling dropped against the almighty U.S. greenback! But wait—what's this? Something called "Light Sweet Crude" was up .31! Dear American Airlines, I haven't the faintest idea what "Light Sweet Crude" is but what an irresistible heading for a personals ad, don't you think? Anyway I'm thrilled that it's up. I might also add that I hope your own stock is through the goddamn roof. Prosperity for all, la-ti-da, la-ti-da. Let's all dance the dollar dance with our fannies in the air.

To be honest, this is the first bar I've set foot inside in five years, and, to be even more honest, I'm not entirely sure why I haven't ordered a drink. At this juncture, fighting the familiar old temptations of the bottle(s) would be like swatting away a wasp while being chewed by an alligator. What's the point?

Eh, resolve. *Resolve*, right: the hayseed cousin of ambition. Doan wanna change the world, jes wanna get the crop in. Mind you, not resolve *against* the booze—I never stopped loving it, even when it was trying to kill me—but, instead, resolve *for* something else, a fixed set of chores yet to be crossed off my list. Look, with the way my brain is wired, it might take me ten years to finish that drink and dammit if I don't have things to do. Still, it's nice to see some old ex-pals. Mr. Galliano there in the back, that tall, lean, goosenecked wallflower. Gentleman Jack out front, that farm-muscled Tennessee bully. Ah, and Smirnoff, Smirnoff, my long-gone true love. We had us a time, didn we? (Cue the barroom piano.) But where the hell did all these other svelte-looking vodkas come from? There's a complete row of them here, out front, preening like pageant contestants in push-up bras. All foreign to me, they must be the new young things, eager and dewy. Anyway, this used to be my crowd. What can I say? I grew up in New Orleans, where cirrhosis of the liver is listed as "Natural Causes" on a death certificate. Was a flailing (flailed?) poet who, corrupted first by Keats and then by Freud, believed that truth was locked up in the attic of the subconscious, demanding blotto liberation. Developed a profound affinity for intoxicated women, not to mention targeted memory loss. My sweaters had holes. My dog died. I missed the bus, I hated the cold, was allergic to dust, can't dance worth a damn. She left me. I left her. Life went on too long. Or like Berryman wrote: "Man, I been thirsty."

And now my eye catches sight of my face reflected in the mirror behind the bar. A raisin at rest. Hair gray, of course (it went gray at thirty), sprawling out from beneath the tweed driver's cap that I've managed to keep on my head since my teens despite all the things that head has done to itself. Face jowly, wrinkled in all the wrong places, the fishhook scar under my eye—this from where Stella cracked me in the face with that water glass—evident even from this distance. The eyes themselves gone increasingly small and crinkly, as if backpedaling their way into my head. According to my mother, I am overweight—one of my favorite of her Post-it notes: "How did you get so fat?"—but in this room, packed with midwesterners, I seem of median girth. If I suggested to the big-bellied fellow next to me, for instance, that his wiener was purple, he would not be able to dispute me without borrowing a makeup mirror; he has doubtlessly not seen his pecker in years.

Oops, he caught me staring. (At his groin, no less.) Turns out his name is Bob, he's in the radon-removal business, he lives in Oshkosh which is where he's trying to return to after a "bullshit" meeting in Houston, thinks the Yankees don't have a prayer this year, and he opened the conversation, rather perceptively, by saying, "Whoa, you're really scribbling away there. Whaddaya, writing your will?" Hahaha, no, says I, an angry letter to American Airlines. "Well, hell, if you want me to sign it, you can make it a petition." (Dear American Airlines, this is actually not a bad idea. Neither is a full-blown riot. Keep me here past roughly eight tomorrow morning, my last shot at making the nuptials, and I'll be the one handing out torches and pitchforks.) "But they're all the same, you know," he said. "United, Delta, US Air. Pick your dick flavor." (Note: He could've said "dictator." His mouth was full of pretzels.) During the course of our exchange Bob rarely took his eyes off the televisions—there are four in range—and peppered his talk with screen-induced non sequiturs, e.g. "Geico. That little lizard is funny." Finally we exhausted our conversational topics and Bob said, "Don't let me keep you from your will. Feel free to leave me the bedroom set." I like Bob. A shame about his purple wiener.

I was never a belligerent drunk, you know. Not a *bad* one, in that sense. Never a fighter, if you discount that one incident with the lawyers which doesn't really qualify as a fight since the lawyers effortlessly squashed me. No, I was at first always a happy drunk, giddy and giggly, in love with whatever or whomever was near me, and then, at some point, a sad drunk, a quiet snuffler, mulling my dumpy ball of wax. It's all cyclical, is what they said at the meetings (which I mostly stopped attending a year ago, though every now and then, when the going gets iffy, I pop in with some donuts): The booze makes you happy but then it makes you sad but you want to be happy again so you drink more, repeat ad infinitum. Or in my case for about thirty years, give or take a bender. If it wasn't for the alcoholic coma I dropped into five years ago (not fun), and the forced re-hab that ensued (ditto), I've no reason to think I wouldn't still be drunk, and that this letter would have already spiraled into even more blathersome blather. Part of the "recovery process" requires apologizing to all those wounded by your drinking, and, for me, Stella Senior got the inaugural call. "What am I supposed to say, Bennie?" she said. Silence on the line. "What do you want to say?" was what I finally croaked out. "Thanks but no thanks," she said. I felt like a rejected telephone solicitor. Click.

I'm reminded now, amidst this beery hubbub, watching a web of conversations spin itself through the room (they're all talking about you, dear American Airlines, and I'm afraid your name is mud), from Oshkosh Bob to the babyfat coed in the UMASS t-shirt doing Cuervo shots with her boyfriend (wheee!), on down the bar to the apparent honeymooners who unsuccessfully ordered champagne, to the mustachioed guy telling the unamused bartender, "Know what TSA stands for? Thousands Standing Around, get it?" and then me, here at the corner, nursing my gone-flat club soda while bobbing atop this frothy sea of chatter: The worst part of sobriety is the silence. The lonesome, pressurized silence. Like the way sound falls away when you're choking. Even when I drank alone, the vodka provided me with a kind of soundtrack—a rhythm, channeled voices, a brain crowded with noise and streaming color, the rackety blurred clutter of my decrepitude. At the meetings everyone talks about how much more vivid life is without the booze, but I think, though I never say, that vivid is the wrong word. Life is rather more *clear*. I'm supposed to be thankful for that clarity, I know, for being freed from that dissonant interior music, from all those flatulent trumpets in my brain, and for finally being able to see life as it is, me as I am. Lookit the world and its blinding rays of light, feel the warmth on my new skin. I'm supposed to be thankful, I know, for being finally shucked down to the core of me. But forgive me, I can't help it: Thanks but no thanks.

I've got to get out of here.

———

HOW BANEFULLY PERFECT. I huffed my way back to K8 where I settled myself safely into one of these torturous gray chairs only to discover, upon cracking Alojzy's book, that Walenty is getting sauced with some new friends. Out of the frying pan, into the fire.

The men were drinking German beer and were welcoming to the point of suspicion. They were already drunk, at lunchtime, and many spoke in slurred, Serb-inflected accents which were difficult for Walenty to understand.

(He'd secured a grip on Italian during his long recovery at the Allied hospital in Rome, when the doctors kept operating and reoperating on his brain, but it was a loose grip.)

Others were foreign sailors whose Italian was more halting than his, but the sailors kept to the café's edges, focusing on their drinking with the seriousness of great athletes. Unfamiliar words whirred past Walenty but the warm beer was like nectar and the men were grinning and slapping their legs and falling from their chairs so Walenty nodded and smiled and when the men raised their glasses, which was often, he raised his as well, toasting indecipherable causes. To peace or more slaughter, to beer or death, to what is past or to come, he was never quite certain. *Alla Salute*.

To bring you up to speed, as they say, Walenty has been roaming Trieste since his morning coffee, overwhelmed by sunlit thoughts of the girl from the train station café. (Cartwheels across his heart, that's what she's doing.) He presumes this is owing to the kindness she showed him that morning, something unseen by him for many years. In 1939, when the Soviets invaded, he watched an old man in his village interrupt the beating of a twelve-year-old boy by shooting one of the boy's Russian assailants in the back with an antique hunting rifle. The old man was immediately killed, of course, machine-gunned into two equal pieces, and when the remaining soldier shouted for four men to come out to remove the old man's body, at least forty villagers trickled out from the doorways. That, Walenty thinks, was the last genuine moment of kindness he could recall. On a boxcar headed to a gulag in northern Kazakhstan, he watched a pregnant woman suckle a starving and half-frozen man at her breast but he would not classify this as kind since the man forced himself upon the woman. She was too weary to resist and after a while closed her eyes and absently stroked his hair. In any case, Walenty now finds himself, lightheaded, in this seaside bar across from a wooden pier in Trieste they call the Molo Audace:

> One of the men, bearish and otherwise fierce-looking, with a black mustache draping his mouth almost completely, began to dance, a solitary *Šetnja*

(I haven't the foggiest what a *Šetnja* is; some type of dance, obviously.)

> that took him around and around the room. When he would encounter chairs or tables he would kick them away with comic aggravation, and everyone howled in delight save the pale she-dwarf who ran the café and whose squeaky protests were swiftly shouted down by demands for more beer.

(Ayyy . . . Alojzy is not this clunkish a writer. "She-dwarf"? Jesus. His translator is merely *verklempt*. Possibly incompetent, too. *Traduttore, traditore*, as the Italian pun goes: *translator, traitor*. Or rather, in this case [no pun extended]: *traduttore, minchione: translator, dumbass*.)

> Soon he came to Walenty and offered his arm. His intent seemed anything but insulting yet still Walenty hesitated. This bear had earned stout laughter for kicking away chairs and tables and, overencouraged, might be seeking to sustain the laughter by dropping the crippled newcomer to the floor. The bear would appear generous but clumsy while Walenty thrashed dumbly on the floorboards. Yet the bear was gently insistent and the other men were clapping and nodding yes so Walenty hooked his arm into the bear's and

away they went, dancing grand circles amidst the disheveled barroom. There was no music save the bear's murmury singing, so it was difficult to keep time, but around and around they went until they had exhausted the confines of the little café and they spilled onto the stones outside. All the men and even the blond dwarf followed them out into the sunlight and were soon clapping a rhythm. Startled children ran to watch them and fishermen stared blankly from the pier. The bear was smiling as he sang, closing his eyes as if to recall, with great force of will, something intensely private and peaceful, and Walenty, inspired, did the same. He scoured his mind but it dispensed him only a single image: the girl from the train station café bending to set down his coffee, the cup trembling musically on the saucer. It was not merely the freshest vision in his head, sprung to the forefront by virtue of its newness, or the most beautiful, or the most vivid, but rather the only vision in his head, like a night sky lit by just a single white star. His mind's near-emptiness made him dizzy, and twice he almost fell, but the bear held him tight by the arm and, with his giant head thrown back and his eyes clamped shut still, sang unknown words that filled the hollows of Walenty's mind as food fills a starving man's belly.

Which reminds me, I'm hungry.

– – – –

IF I'M CALCULATING the time difference correctly, the rehearsal dinner is about to begin in L.A. The table is set with one chair—mine—having been removed, the place settings tightened to conceal an absence going now on twenty-eight years. Though, as Stella Jr. told me, it's technically not a rehearsal dinner: "More like a pre-ceremony get-together" at a "little Alice Waters-y place" on Melrose, is what she said. Well, Stella Jr. always was a good eater. We considered her a prodigy for never spitting out mashed avocado and I swear to God she once ate an anchovy. My presence there tonight was her idea—a way to reacquaint ourselves, so to speak, before the hoopla of the "wedding." (Those damn quotation marks I keep horseshoeing around that word would probably offend her but I don't know what else to do. Their invitation deemed it a "commitment ceremony" but I can't bring myself to ape that hollowed-out language which smacks of a neutered Spivak pronoun or somesuch.) Tonight was her compromise, her way of sorta-maybe agreeing to allow me to walk her down the aisle. "Why don't you come Friday, Bennie?" she asked me on the phone. "Can you? It's just a little too weird for me to say yes now and then have you show up fifteen minutes before the ceremony. It's been a long time, y'know? I won't be *auditioning* you—nothing like *that*. It's just that I'd prefer to have a real face-to-face conversation with you before you trot me down the aisle. That's fair, right? I mean . . . what if you're a Republican?" We laughed together at that one, which felt good—a squirt of oil in the decayed & rusted joints of our bond.

Dear American Airlines, you should've seen me when the invitation arrived. My original thought was that it was some kind of cruel joke from Stella Sr.—her poisonous & long-simmered response to my attempt to make amends of five years ago. I was so obviously dumbfounded—turning the invitation over in my hands as if it would make more sense upside-down (ʎuoɯǝɹǝɔ ʇuǝɯʇıɯɯoɔ), checking and rechecking the envelope's address—that my dumpling Aneta, who delivered the mail to me at my desk, asked if a letter had been misdelivered. There was a bubble of hope in her voice because a misdelivered letter meant that she might have cause to knock at the door of our downstairs neighbor, a heavy-metal guitarist I call Minideth because, when I met him, he was wearing a t-shirt emblazoned with the word Megadeth and because he was then, as now, no more than five feet tall. Aneta is rip-roaringly fond of Minideth despite the callous heartbreak he delivered her when he failed to acknowledge the plate of pierogies she once left, tremblingly, outside his door. I tried explaining to her that in New York no one trusts gifts and/or unattended food and that anyway she doesn't want to get tangled up with a rock 'n' roller, even a profoundly small one. (They're not like dogs, I explained. The bite of a small dog is the same as the bite of a big one.) A displaced farmgirl, Aneta has yet to develop the hard outer shell of cynicism that urban life demands—she is pure, exposed nougat. When the Times Square handbillers force a flyer into her hands she stops and reads it *in toto* and then hands it back with a sincere "thank you" which sometimes elicits an equally sincere "fuck you" from the handbillers. My mother and I used to bang the floor with the butt end of a broomstick whenever Minideth cranked up the amp volume while practicing—bruisy, barely muffled *ch-ch-chunk-chunk* riffs followed by orgasmically shrieksome solos—until one day Aneta scolded us. *A painter! A poet!* she said. *Complaining about another artist!* We relented without argument—less ashamed than flattered, I think, to be called artists, considering that both our creative spigots went dry years ago. I might add that it's truly difficult not to be heartplucked at seeing Aneta go dreamy & gooey at the sound of Minideth practicing—not to want Minideth to be telegraphing his unspoken, fuzzboxed love from one floor below. In those moments Aneta clicks off the television and, clutching a pillow to her chest, sits in reverent silence on the couch beside my mother, whose sour expression evidences a kind of aural indigestion but who puts up with it anyway. A couple weeks back I asked Miss Willa why. LOVE IS LOVE, she wrote on a Post-it. I scoffed, and told her that was a meaningless tautology. She shrugged.

"No, the letter is for me," I told Aneta, rereading the invitation. Still puzzling over my demeanor, she asked if it was bad news. "No," I said, "the opposite—I think." For the rest of the day I was unable to work or concentrate on anything, even dinner which I typically prepare for Miss Willa and myself. (I picked up some frozen Salisbury steaks from Gristede's which my mother refused to acknowledge until I transferred her dinner from the compartmentalized plastic tray, but even then she just picked limply at the mushrooms.) My emotions kept see-sawing: For a while I would feel anguished and stung, as if an old wound had been reopened, a scab scraped from my flesh, after which I'd feel elated and hope-swollen, as if I'd found the first pale crumb of a trail leading back to my life. Mostly, though, I was terrified. For decades I'd kept the sorrows & joys of that ex-life locked safely away, first by drinking, mixing passive self-pity with ice and vodka, and then later by the daily labor of *not* drinking. I don't mean to suggest, melodramatically, that I ceased to *function* because of it all—over the years I wrote & published & held jobs & maintained a dwindling number of friendships & even tucked into those years a laughably brief and impetuous marriage that isn't worth discussing. But a part of me had been amputated by what transpired between me and my Stellas—if I may continue, haplessly, in my fumbling for metaphors. And now here, courtesy of an embossed envelope, was my severed limb come back to me, the shredded ligaments still curling outward from its raw and oozing red core, the arteries still faintly pulsing.

Three shaky days later, on a Saturday afternoon, I called Stella Jr.; there was an RSVP number on the invitation, which I ran through an internet search engine to ensure it didn't belong to Stella Sr. I didn't know even the first words to say to her: *This is your father?* That struck me as a false title, even more fraudulent than Aneta deeming me a poet. (Ex-father, ex-poet, ex-drunk: Everything I am gets prefaced with an ex.) Therefore, "This is Bennie," I said, when I hooked her on the phone after several hangups on her voicemail. "Bennie who?" she said, and inside I buckled. So it *had*, after all, been a vicious trick of Stella Sr.'s. "Bennie . . . Ford," I said, and then the voice said, "Oh, God. Let me get Stel," and I heard the voice whisper, "I think it's your dad," followed by a lengthy silence. With a prick, it occurred to me that I had no clue what my daughter's voice might sound like. I had only ever heard her coo and cry when she was the small pink creature I called Speck. I, who lived on words, who had eaten them, drunk them, dreamt them, created them, who even now still inhaled and exhaled them, transforming them, in my translations, as a body converts oxygen to carbon dioxide, had vanished from her life before words had entered it. The one thing I might've given her, I didn't.

"Bennie," she said. The voice was lilting, sunny, freewheeling, recognizably Californian. "Wow."

Not knowing what to say, I said, "Maybe you can imagine, but I don't know what to say."

"You got the invitation."

"It was very nice."

"Mom and I went round and round about that," she said. "I won." I had to make a quick little mental leap to connect "Mom" with Stella Sr., as my brain wasn't equipped with that particular equal sign. Mom. The word flipflopped inside my head: Wow. "How *are* you, Bennie?" she said.

"How are *you?*" I replied.

"I'm good, I'm great." We went on like this for a bit. "Hey," she said, "this feels like a weird question to ask—I guess it *is* a weird question, sorry—but is Grandma still alive? I heard she had a stroke or something."

Grandma = Miss Willa, another mental leap across sharp rocks. Mom = Stella. Everyone had a stock role to play but me: The part of the Bennie will be played by Bennie. "She's alive, yes," I told her. "She's in the next room, in fact, watching an *Iron Chef* rerun. The stroke calmed her down a bit. I don't know how much you know about her. Kind of a yin and yang to it."

An anxious, brittle laugh. "I don't know *what* to say to that."

"Let's just say she used to be more of a handful. Hey, look," I said, sensing in her laughter a wave to surf in on, "I'd like to come to your wedding."

"Seriously? That's fantastic." Genuine-sounding glee.

"And I'm looking forward to meeting the young man." This, of course, was knuckleheaded on two disproportionate counts. One: "*the young man*"? What was that—a flaccid Robert Young impersonation? I winced as the words spilled across my lips. Second:

"Oh, Bennie, yikes. Syl is a woman. I'm gay. I'm sorry, you couldn't have known . . ."

"No, no, hey . . . groovy." *Groovy*, that's what I said. In ransacking my mind for something to say that wouldn't come across as shocked or disapproving or priggish or homophobic, none of which I was, or had any right to be, I burped the word "groovy," which I don't believe I'd uttered since the age of fourteen and even then with a lacquer of irony. Yet as inappropriate and pot-perfumed as *groovy* was, it was far superior to the next batter in my mental dugout: I almost popped out a blithe & sincere "Whatever floats your boat," which was about the worst I could've said outside of citing our mutual love of chicks as evidence of the DNA bond. *Groovy*. Even now, however, with all this time to consider it, I can't tell you what an ideal reaction would have been. Maybe the empty wisdom of Miss Willa's Post-it note: LOVE IS LOVE.

"Mom still hasn't wrapped her head around it but she's trying," she said. "You'll adore Syl, she's totally wonderful." Would I? It hardly mattered. We talked a bit more. Speck did catering for film sets, and had apparently achieved some success because she referenced movie stars by their first names and

61

lamented her busy schedule with the *dégagé* calm of someone who has everything entirely under control. She'd met Sylvana, an entertainment lawyer, at a "wrap party" two years ago and they were considering having children(!). Adopting *of course*, she said. For their "honeymoon"—does that require quotation marks? Why am I compelled to write about my daughter's nuptials in the manner of a Zagat review?—they were going to Mali and Senegal, where Sylvana had arranged to visit some adoption agencies. Stella Jr. found the prospect of parenting more daunting & fearsome than Syl did, to which I could offer no words of counsel. Syl was a "big fan" of my old poetry and she and Stella Jr. wondered what had happened to my writing, to which I responded, falsely I suppose, that I often wondered that same thing myself. Their bookshelves held a couple of my translations, too, but Stella Jr. apologized for what she gently termed their "neglect" of Eastern European writing. Syl was really big into Third World lit, Stella Jr. said, mentioning a couple of postcolonial writers from the Indian subcontinent with whom I was familiar only as vowelly names on book spines. She and Sylvana loved L.A.—she admitted this was a contrarian viewpoint—and lived downtown which rather extended the contrarian streak. At times our conversation was so light and easy that it disturbed me; with that much water under the bridge, it was hard to believe the bridge could still be standing. Finally I told her I had a request I expected her to deny, and, frankly, I would understand her denying it more easily than I would her granting it. But I wanted to ask.

"Shoot," she said.

I asked if she would let me walk her down the aisle . . . if, of course—here I stammered—there was an aisle.

"Oh, wow, Bennie. That's a jump." What followed was a silence that could be classified as huge. "Mom would flip." Another silence. "We . . . we were planning on walking down together, I guess. Jesus, Bennie, this has been so . . . so nice but that seems like zero to sixty in an awfully short time." (An automotive analogy—ah, my daughter was L.A. through and through.) "Let me to talk to Syl, okay? After all we're in this together." I told her not to worry, that it was an undeserved longshot, a selfish dream lobbed from a long-lost past. Inviting me was more than enough, I didn't mean to push. Silly me, etc. "I just need to think about it," Speck told me.

I can't say precisely why but after I hung up the phone I put my head in my hands and wept—hoarse, dry sobs I was unable to stifle or control.

An hour later Stella Jr. called back. "Syl thinks it's a gorgeous idea," she said. "That it's beautifully *circular.* Another twist—wait, how did she put this?—of unconventional conventionality. My God, it's going to be a day." That's when she proposed her compromise plan—that we'd meet tonight, at the non-rehearsal dinner, which by my estimate, dear American Airlines, should currently be in the appetizer stage. Insert your own cursewords here. Make sure they're your favorites because they're all for you.

When I went to tell Miss Willa that I'd spoken to her granddaughter, whose mysterious estrangement from us she'd ceased commenting upon twenty years ago, I found her drafting an epic, nine-page Post-it note message with her mother's old copy of the *Picayune's Creole Cookbook* (1901 edition) cracked open before her on the TV tray. "Miss Willa," I said, but she held up a narrow, vein-braided hand to shush me before resuming her labors. When she finally finished she handed me the pile of yellow stickies with a stern nod. I read them one by one. With painstaking care, she'd transcribed, in her wobbly avian scrawl, a passage from the cookbook—a rebuke, I gathered quickly, for the last few nights of me glumly serving her frozen dinners. It went like this:

THE SERVING IS
THE MOST IMPORTANT

AFTER COOKING. NEVER
CROWD A DISH INTENDED

FOR AN INVALID. SPREAD
A DAINTY NAPKIN ON

THE SALVER. ARRANGE
THE FOOD IN A MOST

APPETIZING WAY, LAY
A ROSEBUD OR A

FLOWER FRESH FROM
THE GARDEN ON THE

SALVER, AND BRING
IN THE DAINTY,

TEMPTING MORSEL
WITH A HAPPY, CHEERY

SMILE, THOUGH YOUR
HEART MAY BE SINKING.

"But, Mother," I said. "That's what I'm trying to tell you. My heart isn't sinking."

- - - -

THAT NIGHT I bought my ticket via www.aa.com, your cluttery but operable website. It was a "Net SAAver" special—for, as I believe I've mentioned, $392.68. It doesn't soften my stance one bit to admit that I liked the nice price. One of your competitors wanted a full hundred dollars more. When I clicked "Purchase and Confirm" I felt a shudder run through my body—somewhere between giddy and forlorn, hopeful and frightened, not an entirely pleasant sensation but not unpleasant either. For a long while afterward I remained at my desk in the unlit room, smoking cigarette after cigarette while the computer's lava-lamp screensaver threw undulating colors into the thickening & billowing bluish haze. Something terrible must've happened that night—I remember the city filling with sirens.

Drunk, he was unable to walk. The false limb unsteadied him enough while sober; but after glass after glass of beer, Walenty found himself mortally imbalanced, clinging to chairs and tables to stay upright. By now it was very late at night and the black sea out beyond the Molo Audace was calm and moonflecked. The men were saying their good-byes and some were saying ugly things about their wives asleep at home and the work they had to do the next day. Walenty had no place to sleep and he blurted this fact, laughingly, to the bear, who laughed, too—so uproariously that tears ran down his reddened cheeks. Everyone thought it hilarious except the sober dwarf behind the bar who ordered the bear to escort Walenty to a *pensione* on the hill below the cathedral.

With Walenty supported by the bear, they tottered through the streets howling songs in their native tongues, a typhoon of slurred baritone babble. When they awakened the old woman who ran the *pensione* she scolded them harshly and even spat at the bear whose subsequent laughter only enraged her further, provoking another blast of spittle. There was a gray mustache above her lip so slight it could be mistaken for dirt. One of her eyes was blind and milky, and her nubby fingers were sootblacked; one of the fingers, Walenty noticed, was missing a nail. Examining her closer, he realized she was not as old as one might think. She was rather, like the rooms she rented, overused.

The room was small and moldy and the vast stains splashed on the walls suggested a long-receded flood. With the old-looking woman standing in the doorway, the bear helped Walenty onto the bed, its mattress thin as a cracker, and kissed him and pinched his cheek in the way of Italian men. As the bear left, the woman again spat at him and he ran down the hallway hooting with a laughter that continued even after he was free outside. Lying on the bed, Walenty could hear the laughs spilling down the cobblestoned hill. He slept with his leg attached and was dazzled by placid dreams.

He awoke the next morning just before dawn; even after a buoyant night of drinking, he was still a model soldier. The birdsongs surprised him—the sound was like that of a thousand music boxes being played at once. Lying there, he could not recall the last time he had heard birds. The Germans, went the rumor, had driven them out of Poland, and they'd been wholly absent during the Anzio fighting. Once Walenty had seen a black vulture tearing at the groin of a dead British infantryman. The men had tried to ignore it until they saw a recognizable organ in the vulture's beak and then one of the soldiers, an otherwise calm and stoical Varsovian who had taught music before the war, stood up and shot it. Later they discovered it was called locally *Avvoltoio monaco* and had been thought to be extinct.

When Walenty sat up in bed he was astonished at how good he felt. He had never been a drinker because he was oversensitive to the following day's aftereffects, and he'd expected, darkly, to awaken craving morphine. Now, craving coffee instead, he remembered the girl at the café and ran his fingers through his hair. He had never been so happy in his life.

Dear American Airlines, you miserable fucks, I'm going to keep writing. I'm going to keep writing and writing and writing and writing and you're going to keep reading and reading because for the first time in my life it wasn't me that blew it—it was you. Since you've stranded me here for at best this day and this night, blaming mute thunder and dry rain and fugitive winds, Acts of God my ass—since you've trapped me here alone, caught between the dregs of one life and the debris of another, then you will sit here beside me, goddamn you, you will sit here beside me and you will listen to me, you will listen for as long as your boot sticks me to the floor, for as long as you hold me here, for as long as my voice holds out, I'm going to keep writing, goddamnit, we have a long night ahead and I'm not going to stop.

- - - -

I MAY, HOWEVER, stop smoking. Fueling my lungs is getting to be an onerous chore. One of the TSA screeners has made it his playful task to discourage me, by unrelentingly pulling me aside for *de trop* inspection whenever I re-pass through the security checkpoint, and while I wouldn't confess this to him, it's working. He's a boisterous senior with a snowy crewcut who probably used to work in industrial sales. "Them things gonna kill ya, tiger," he says to me. (Why "tiger"? An endearing midwesternism, I suppose. Grrr.) "Well," I say, as he runs his wand beneath my armpits, my groin, "I wish they'd hurry up. I've been waiting forty years." It occurs to me that jolly cracks about suicide are taboo at the checkpoints but this one is pretty oblique and anyway my ex-salesman seems to get the joke. Life didn't drop him where he expected to be at his age either. He liked Ike and switched to margarine and opened his hymnal to the page as directed but here he is anyway, still shoveling snow and still polishing a nametag, a thousand miles from Florida. *Hast thou not poured me out as milk*, wailed Job, *and curdled me like cheese?* "You think about what I said," he calls after me. Old friend, you don't know the half of it.

Outside beside the gray Skycap Services hutch is where I smoke. Across the street from me is a train platform and a parking garage where rust has left vertical stains on the concrete and steel panels, and, beyond the garage, the giant and completely booked Hilton hotel with its monolithic face of black windows that reminds me, not warmly, of the architecture of Soviet-era Bulgaria. The crowd of smokers keeps growing denser and I wonder if the tension of being stranded at O'Hare is luring some reformed smokers back into the fold; I'm increasingly getting hit on for smokes. The crowd keeps getting surlier, too. I heard one man announce that there were no hotel rooms to be had unless you went south of Gary, Indiana. Another smoker, a postmenopausal woman with a trademark Virginia Slims voice, added that this was partly due to a medical information technologies convention that's being held downtown. Well, whadyaknow. Another fella chimed in that there are no rental cars to be had, either—not a single sedan in all of Chicagoland. "I guess we're snowed in for the night," someone said. "Except there's no snow," someone else retorted (stealing, I suspect, the first guy's punchline), and then the whole gang laughed the most mirthless laugh you've ever heard.

"Hey-ho, here he comes again," my TSA screener said to me on my way back in. "Still kicking."

"Kicking and screaming," I said.

"You get 'em, tiger," he said, this time letting me pass by unhindered.

Along with the smoking, choosing my latest perch is also growing more difficult. It seems mathematically improbable but I feel certain that I've sampled the O'Chairs at every one of the gates here—finding none satisfactory, of course. I'm an airport Goldilocks! Currently I'm at H6, where I'm seated beneath a sign displaying an illustration of an airplane beside an encircled question mark. It seems to signify nothing. (I would know if there were an information booth here because I'm sitting precisely where it would be.) Or, from another angle, to signify everything: immobile planes, meet festering questions.

Anyway, no one seems to notice it. I should note, for the record, that throughout the afternoon I intermittently inquired of the attendant at the American Airlines desk—above which this sign should probably be hanging—just when I might expect to soar away from here but she never could say. (Once it was a he, but same story.) After a while I stopped doing so because it seemed futile plus I was beginning to feel like a stalker. It's never comforting when someone says to you, "You need to try to calm down, sir." But the attendants are facing a lot of heat so I don't hold anything against them. Certainly I wouldn't be able to do their jobs. By now I'd have jabbed my fingers, Stooges-style, into the eyes of a dozen disgruntled passengers, me included. You pinheads ain't flying the friendly skies. Pow! This is America, sit the fuck down.

Stray thought: All day now I've been thinking that O'Hare evokes Purgatory but I've been dismissing this perceived likeness as the product of an addled mind. Yet now I'm not so sure. The figurative sometimes congeals with the literal. Consider the view from my chair at H6: Sprawled 'round me is a crowd of temporary refugees waiting, waiting, yawning, drumming fingers on kneecaps, asking cellphones what they did to deserve this, rereading *The Da Vinci Code* to keep from having to stare at the carpet. Even the million-miler business travelers have run out of steam—the suited laptop jockey beside me is playing a version of solitaire on his computer and the way he's sighing and petulantly flicking his fingerpad leads me to believe that this is his last refuge of mental and/or physical activity. Airports are usually so fluid—people moving like fish in schools. But movement is scarce here tonight: stragglesome wanderers, looking purposeless and disattached, strolling for the sake of motion. Mothers are unduly snapping at children. Middle-aged men are learning to use the unexplored features of their digital wristwatches. A semi-punished lot, all of us: imprisoned within a pause, desperate to ascend.

Not to mention that everything here is colored in vary-ing shades of purgatorial gray: the slate of the ceiling tiles, the wet-concrete hue of the columns, the floor tiles mottled like dusty gravel. The light pale and diffuse, a fluorescent mist. As in Dante's *Purgatorio*, no one casts a shadow. *Time passes on, and we perceive it not.* The escalators move us from one mountain-ous terrace to another. *What negligence, what standing still is this.* And instead of Dante's angels, with their flaming swords deprived of points, we are guarded by TSA screeners like my new friend advising me to repent from the death-lust of Lucky Strikes, marking my forehead with that bleating electronic wand of his as Alighieri's brow was carved at the gates. Con-fess thy sins, tiger: *May pity and justice disburden you soon, that ye may have power to move the wing.* Empty your pockets, please. Empty too thy addled mind.

RAY QUENEAU—formerly a minor god of mine, so far as trans-lating goes; this, of course, back when I actually had gods (now I only have you)—once said that true stories are about food and made-up stories are about love. This line flitted into my mind a few minutes ago as I was chewing a "famous" "Baja" Chipotle Chicken Burrito from the Burrito Beach outlet. (I ac-companied my six-pound burrito—a steaming hippo turd dis-guised as cuisine—with an "Arizona Green Tea," in order, I guess, to completely short-circuit my gastrointestinal recep-tors. Were I, say, a drunk New Orleans attorney, I might leap across the counter to throttle the server for this cement mixer of a dinner, though the homemade gang tattoos sprucing the server's knuckles might give me pause, plus it's not like I didn't have an array of other food-court options. Butter Crust Chi-cagoland Pizza & McFuggets! Fu Manchu Wok Craaaaziness. Aromatherapy smoothies. But the Burrito Beach had the shortest line, hence my hippo turd. When I dumped my uneaten leftovers in the trash, the whole can trembled.)

Anyway, Queneau, me chewing: I was idly skimming this dread letter of mine when my eyes happened to stop on the three blank lines that I left between the tale of Bennie and Stella's first encounter and that of my run-in with the sweet old munchkinette outside advocating slot-machine therapy. Three blank lines: a page break, a smoke break, a visual exhalation after that remembrance of Magazine Street. Don't riffle backwards—I can tell you precisely what I wrote: "I stood there for a long while, my heart a sparkler spraying light across the sidewalk." A nice metaphor, isn't it? If maybe a little dainty & saccharine. Naturally I stole it. Sort of stole it, anyway, from a dead Varsovian poet named Blazej Krawczyk whose posthumous collected poems I translated years ago. The verse, so far as I can recall it, went something like this:

On an empty street, past midnight, you lit my heart's fuse.
I watched, amazed, as my chest
heaved white sparks upon the stones.
I laughed because I had never seen it do that.

But when I looked up you were running. You
glanced only once over your shoulder as you fled.
You could not have heard me say your name. *Katarzyna*.
No. All you could have heard was the blast.
For blocks, every windowpane quivered. Dogs
barked, lights appeared as question marks. But
there was nothing to see. You were gone
and so was I.

How brutal! And of course how common. This Katarzyna performing the romantic equivalent of the old Halloween "ring and run" trick. You can almost hear the clicks of her heels on the rainslicked cobblestones while the poet stands frozen with his poor torso about to explode, the expression on his face collapsing, melting, as the fuse dwindles inward. (Though I doubt Krawczyk would have written those lines had he lived long enough to see suicide bombers dominating the newscrawls . . . the modern evocations—wrecked and repressed Arab youths transforming themselves into hand grenades, into fatal pop-up political ads—are just too godawful ugly. Dear American Airlines, you've got far more pressing personal grievances against the jihadists than I do, but still, notwithstanding what they did to my adopted city, and the hot bejesus they scared out of my mother, the fuckers also soiled a great metaphor. If there is any vengeful comfort available to us, though, consider this: A savvy German scholar calling himself Christoph Luxenberg—a shielding pseudonym—recently concluded that the passages in the Koran promising a bevy of dark-eyed virgins to dead Muslim males is a mistranslation. Read in the original Syriac, the Koran instead promises rare and presumably delicious *white raisins*, which, while mildly tempting in the way of dried fruit, hardly approach the moist allure of seventy-two spread-eagled sweeties beckoning with a curled finger in the way of pulpfiction vixens. Would the jihadists who flew your planes into the twin towers & the Pentagon have licked their lips before impact in the expectation of raisins? Let us not forget that suicide is a profoundly self-interested act. Luxenberg's revelation has lately stiffened my resolve when my translating seems worthless, a chore of lingual accountancy. The right word matters, it says to me. The wrong ones infect, spread disease. Words are everything.)

One thing, however, that I've never been entirely clear about: Did Katarzyna perish in the blast? It's not altogether evident, is it? *Wy byliście nieobecni*, was what Krawczyk wrote: literally, *You were absent*. Krawczyk was three years dead by the time I got to the poem, so I never had the chance to ask. I suppose the answer hinges on whatever emotional luggage you're packing when you encounter the poem. Is the end of love an implosion or an explosion? Was that hussy Katarzyna flattened by shrapnel (metaphorically, of course), hurled face-first to the street, or did the poet's remains float down upon her like flakes of soot, like benign embers hissing in the rivulets of rainwater between the cobblestones?

But then it appears I'm skidding off the runway again. Where was I? Oh yes: the young Me as fizzy sparkler, freckling Magazine Street with my Stellated ecstasy. And then those three blank lines, containing multitudes. That tender, gauzy fade-out. What I'm wondering is why I stopped the story where I did, with that sweet pilfered metaphor that's been jangling about in my pockets for years. (Beyond the obvious reason, I mean: I needed a cigarette.) Unlike Krawczyk's betrayed poet, I didn't go boom that morning. I went back home and mixed a stout nightcap and smoked two or three Luckies before masturbating myself to sleep. Six or seven hours later I helped Charles clean his apartment, bagging beer cans and emptying ashtrays and fielding shit from him for "disappearing all night with that flatchested chick." ("Flatchested?" I said. "You sure? I didn't notice." "You didn't *notice*," he said, with a roll of the eyes. Well, I didn't notice.) Then we went to the Exchange where I got luminously hammered and considered calling Stella—I still had her number in the back pocket of my jeans—but didn't, mostly owing to the presence there of an art student named Valerie who, when she drank gin, tended to get nearsightedly horny, and who happened that night to be drinking gin. Normally I hated talking to her—she was from upstate New York and thought she was doing aesthetic missionary work down South, irrigating the Sahara of the Bozarts—but the saucy things she said under the influence of gin were terribly hard to ignore, e.g. "Gosh, I'm feeling so edible right now." Gulp. So why not finish my story there? Me, the walking, talking sparkler—drunk with new love, but drunker with vodka and erotic *bons mots?* Or for that matter, why not wrap it up a few dark hours later when I stumbled home from Valerie's barefooted because I'd been too drunk to find my shoes? (The next night, when I did finally call Stella, and we talked for three hours, it emerged that I'd been shoe shopping that afternoon. The joke, for weeks after, was that I'd bought new shoes to impress her. Her joke, not mine.)

But then Krawczyk wasn't writing about the beginning of love, let's remember, Bennie. He was writing about the end.

After my and Stella's final argument, kindled by my conjuring of Speck's far-off wedding, naturally I retreated to the Exchange. The typical male drinks heavily in such situations, so I suppose I was typical though toward the far end of the bell curve. To put it mildly I drank my fool head off. I toppled off my barstool and vomited in the bathroom trough and spent much of the evening collapsed against the shoulder of B. B. Mike who goodnaturedly obliged me though not without calling me a drooling homo. Some Uptown cuties slumming it for a bachelorette party sneaked a plastic tiara onto my head—without ever speaking to me, I mean; that's what kind of spectacle I was—which I didn't even know was there until long after I'd left the bar. That must've been four or five hours after my entrance; all I know is that I departed, on foot (Felix the Fat confiscated my keys), and in a light rain, well before last call.

The key was gone. We kept the spare housekey hidden beneath a struggling potted cotton plant in the hallway; the key was for me because I was always forgetting my own keys, or, on rarer occasions like this one, having them taken away from me. I rapped on the door for several minutes—a frantic rat-a-tat—at first as quietly as I could (for Speck's sake), and then with mounting urgency and volume. When that didn't work I pounded the door with the side of my fist. Inside me was a shotgun-patterned anger that even today I can't precisely explain: I was angry at Stella for no longer being in love with me and angry at myself for deserving that unlove. I was boiling in guilt for the . . . for the shambles I was, and with rage for the shambles I thought she'd made of me. I hated her for wanting to leave me even though a part of me wanted to watch her go. I hated her because I loved my daughter and my Stellas could not be wrenched apart. I hated her because the sight of myself reflected in her eyes made me recoil. I hated her because all I'd wanted in life was to fuck and drink and make poems and die young and in the saddle singing yahoo. I hated her because I could abide neither her presence nor her absence. And I hated myself because I was a shitheel father who didn't even *get* the joy of parenthood until six or seven months in when Speck was old enough to react to me, to *reflect* me — which meant Stella was right, that down deep I considered myself the sun, the center of all orbits, my mother's child after all. And I hated myself too because when I drank I became someone else and I loved that someone else while I was him and despised him when I wasn't. And finally I hated everyone/everything because ultimately there was no escape, I was trapped within myself and my life, there was no ending or outcome that wasn't going to hurt me or them or us all. Yet at the same time I didn't or couldn't believe all that. There were words that could fix this, there had to be. We could bandage or bury this night & all the others like it with the right words, by saying them, believing them, crawling inside them together, inhabiting their worn confines, lighting a candle, and growing old within them. And while I punched that door harder and harder — I remember this — I thought of walking my daughter down the aisle on her wedding day. My mind fastened upon that frilly, cast-off vision that had so weirdly, inexplicably led me here, that daydream — no, that sweetened-condensed nightmare — that I'd never actually *had* before stating it aloud (why *would* I have? What man dreams of giving away what he loves to someone else, slicing off and serving a piece of his heart? That's almost like aspiring to be Abraham on Mount Moriah, rearing back with the knife over beloved Isaac. If anything I dreamt of my daughter traveling the world solo, absorbing its Technicolor marvels, writing me lavishly detailed letters from Borneo and Budapest, footloose and earth-soaked and wholly unbothered by the anklebites of marriage, the drowsy bleakness of domesticity)—there in that hallway I fixed upon that sweet, poisonous anti-dream that, in its revealing, had ignited all this, had triggered this end, and as I pounded and kicked the door I said to it: *I'm not a liar Stella I'm not.*

Nothing. I dropped to my knees and punched the door more weakly then put my ear to it to see if I could maybe hear her breathing on the opposite side. That's when I realized I was wearing the plastic tiara. Discovering that reignited my rage and I went outside and around the corner of the house to a spot beneath our bedroom window. A narrow, grassy channel separated our house from the neighboring one—too wide to pass an egg from window to window but slim enough to confidently toss one across. There was no light in our bedroom window above me but of course she was in there, I knew it. Where else could she be? By now the rain had strengthened and I was soaked through. Enraged and intoxicated, and above all else wounded, I stood below our window and with all that was in me I bellowed out her name.

Almost instantly, however, I went silent—struck mute by the interior echo. "Oh shit," I finally said aloud. Had Stella been named anything else, and/or had we lived in any other city besides New Orleans, my desperate call would have been just my desperate call. In that alternate universe the neighbors might have peeked from behind the curtains but they wouldn't have laughed or, worse, joined in. But you simply cannot shout the name Stella while standing under a window in New Orleans and hope for anything like an authentic or even mildly earnest moment. Literature had beaten me to this moment, had staked its flag here first, and there was nothing I could do outside in that soupy, rain-drenched alleyway that could rise above sad parody. Perhaps if she'd been named Beatrice, or Katarzyna—maybe then my life would have turned out differently. Maybe then my voice would have roused her to the window, maybe then I could have told her that I was sorry, that I could be a better man, that I couldn't promise I knew everything it meant but I loved her. Instead I stared up at that black window, shutmouthed and impotent, blinking and reblinking my eyes to flush out the rainwater. "Stella," I whispered. The French have an expression: "Without literature life is hell." Yeah, well. Life with it bears its own set of flames.

WHEW. ME AGAIN. As to the three blank lines immediately preceding this: Dear American Airlines, you don't want to know what they contain. Suffice it to say that I no longer possess that six-pound "famous" chipotle chicken burrito, physiologically speaking, and the evidence suggests that I may have been stricken with an O'Hare strain of *E. coli* that may soon annihilate me in a way the vodka never could. I know why the trash can trembles.

But help me out here. For the past ten minutes or so, among other activities, I've been pondering why airport bathrooms hardly ever feature graffiti. Truckstop bathrooms serve much the same purpose—as pitstops for travelers on the go—yet their walls are almost always festooned with rich commentary. *Jesus saves!* (The rejoinder: *But Satan invests.*) *Don't look for a joke here, it's in your hand. Please don't toss cigarette butts in the toilet, it makes them hard to light. John 3:16.* (Rejoinder: *Matthew 3:20—just missed you.*) Etc. And my personal favorite, which I saw scrawled on a condom machine in an Allentown, PA, truckstop: *Insert baby for refund.* In high school, a friend and I actually dialed a "For a Good Time, Call" number spied on the bathroom wall of an Uptown New Orleans po' boy joint. When a female voice answered we threw the receiver back and forth like a fiery ember until her plaintive, patient hellos got the best of me. "Yes," I said, appropriating, for whatever reason, the voice of TV's Maxwell Smart, "I'm calling in reference to a good time." "Oh, God," she said. "My ex-husband Bobby wrote that where he used to work. I thought he'd scratched it out—he said he did." At this point the conversation should have ended with an apology from me and the buzz of a dial tone from her, but without so much as an awkward pause she asked if I'd had the roast beef and gravy (the restaurant's claim to glory) and I said no, I'd had a peacemaker (fried oysters & shrimp), which she said was okay but not nearly as good as the roast beef and gravy so long as you got it "dressed" but not with pickles because pickles were gross. The conversation continued like this, lazily, while my buddy lay on the couch asphyxiating himself with pillows—he was certain I was en route to high-speed carnal glory the moment he heard me venture that "sometimes dressed is good." After a while I abandoned the Maxwell Smart voice, which must have clued her in to my age because swiftly thereafter she begged off the phone. I learned several lessons from that call: (1) that the world was a much more lonesome & wicked place than I'd realized (her *ex-husband?*); and (2) that my native New Orleans, where dialing a number found on a bathroom wall yielded you a discussion about po' boys, was a truly weird city. (Allow me now to make the sign of the cross to bless its drowned soul. I remember watching the news after Katrina hit and thinking—outside of the hot grief I felt for all those homegrown refugees and old ladies being plucked from rooftops and, Jesus, that poor kid being stripped of his snowpuff dog—thinking: There it goes, my past. Washing away in the flood, godspeed.)

Really, though: It doesn't make a lick of sense, this lack of wordage in the restroom stalls. Airports are petri dishes for boredom, rage, nicotine withdrawal, and gastrointestinal discomfort—the presumed nuclei of anonymous bathroom verse—and yet the walls here are as blank as a dead man's eyeball. The only marks at all are random scratches that I'm at a loss to explain, unless jetsetting circus tigers use these loos. You would think that some enterprising and disaffected soul would be inspired to write something along, say, these lines: *I fucked in Florida, I fucked in Maine. / I fucked for three days on the coast of Spain. / But I'll never be happy, never be free / until I fuck this airline, like it fucked me.* But no, nothing. Not a sign of life in these restrooms save the sounds and smells of businessmen voiding the fruits of their expense accounts. Perhaps it's true what they say. Maybe poetry really is dead.

Mine certainly is. The last poem I published was in 1995; the last poem I wrote, not counting the ditty above, came maybe a year later. It would be false modesty to say no one noticed though just barely. Mostly, it was an amicable split. That great old line of Larkin's—"I haven't given up poetry; poetry has given me up"—doesn't apply here. No, exhausted from decades of quarreling, we each gave up on the other. My mother still hopes for a reunion, goading me with a stick rather than a carrot: NO ONE, said one Post-it, REMEMBERS THE TRANSLATOR. "Oh, Miss Willa," I whined back, "no one remembers the poets anymore either." Officially (by which I mean, when familiar bartenders asked), my reason for quitting was that poetry had finally struck me as a futile weapon against the world. Iambic pentameter is no sword with which to slay evil or even ennui. That sort of thing. And though I sometimes believe that, usually I don't. All I have to do is remember the streaming red blood that poems—other writers' poems—drew from me over the years. The way certain poems guided me through life like blue runway lights. Or more accurately like pinball bumpers.

My mother awards herself credit for what she terms my "artistic bent"—at this point, a nice way to describe my toolbox of personality disorders. For letting me, as a toddler, wallow in piles of books while she sat before her easel in City Park. For being moral and sophisticated enough to ban "Little Black Sambo" from my bedtime reading. For subscribing to *Highlights* and helping me write my first published work, a letter to the creators of the "Doctor Fate and Hourman" comic books (which, now that I think about it, was a letter of complaint—one might say I've been working toward this moment all my life). The "artist" in me, she's always claimed, descends from my Desforge roots—is derived exclusively from the sap from her family tree. All I inherited from the Ford *né* Gniech side, according to Miss Willa, was my nappy hair and my inexplicable love of consonants.

As with most matters, she's wrong. My father didn't read for pleasure—nothing about English provided him pleasure, and Polish lit was nearly impossible to come by in New Orleans—but in his mind was a storehouse of remembered Polish verse: Mickiewicz, Witwicki, Slowacki, all the nineteenth-century Romantics. On nights when my mother was "away" (hospitalized, primarily, or taking night-school classes in Japanese pen-and-ink drawing or Advanced Bridge, or communing with her revolving cast of "best" friends who would invariably "turn" on her), he would lie next to me at bedtime and recite reams of lilting, beautifully incomprehensible poems: *Gdybym ja była słonecykiem na niebe, Nie świeciłabzm, jak tzlko dla ciebie.* For me, it was lingual white noise, those Polish consonant endings like evanescent static, whispers of *shhh*, the rise and fall of octosyllabic verses rocking me to sleep as pitching seas lull a sailor. Perhaps he felt he had nothing else to give me—he could no more decipher a volume of Uncle Remus than he could a Greek bible—or perhaps (my preference) he relished those sparse and covert moments when he could speak his mother tongue freely, and could share it with me. Miss Willa, convinced he was lamenting his life with her whenever he spoke Polish, and piercingly ashamed of his Polack origins, forbade his speaking it in the house. By this time he had quit his exterminator job and was working at an automotive shop on Poydras Street—because it specialized in imports, my mother tended to refer to him as a "Rolls-Royce specialist"—and beside me at night he smelled of motor sludge and cigarettes and whatever acidic solvents he scrubbed his hands with so that my mother wouldn't fuss about his oil-encrusted fingers. My fond memories of him are few: He worked, he ate, he enjoyed the *Lawrence Welk Show* for the polkas though any moving images sufficed, he fixed the sink when it was leaking and tended to the fireplace on Christmas morning while my mother buzzed about the living room demanding to be told the day was *perfect*. But in those dark, poem-strewn moments he was nothing short of magical—a wizard conjuring forth my dreams with his clandestine and incantatory language.

Without stretching the matter too far, you could say that poetry raised me. By the time I hit adolescence, my father was a gray shadow passing soundlessly through the house, the ghost of a martyred handyman, and my mother remained, as before, a case for a psychological bomb squad. They were less parents than cellmates and we all privately marked off the days of our confinement. My father won this grim contest by dying when I was fifteen—the victim of an unexpected heart attack that struck him in his sleep. For so sudden a death, and at such a pregnable age for me, it was a strangely unemotional passing. He was only forty-eight but his death felt like that of a nursing-home patient who'd been bedridden and cancer-racked for years: an act of mercy, a gift rather than a theft. I don't remember even crying at his funeral. I felt as if I was waving goodbye as he embarked upon a new and better adventure. Send me a postcard, *Tata*. Be brave.

In any case, I found myself nearing manhood with scant instruction on living, so for lessons I turned to books, and in books of poetry—particularly those of Baudelaire, Keats, Neruda, Lorca, Yeats, the Beats—I discovered the life I thought I wanted: heart-fueled, reckless, close to the bone, earthly existence set to a rolling, overspilling boil. Let me say upfront that this is no way to read poetry. When Neruda writes about how great it would be "to go through the streets with a green knife letting out yells" until you die of the cold, he does not intend for you to take him literally. The dearth of green knives in your neighborhood cutlery emporium ought to be clue number one, but just you try explaining that to a vulnerable seventeen-year-old. Because I loved the way words & images bounced through my head when I read poetry, the way it *impelled* my life as nothing else did, revved it like a floored gas pedal, I began writing it.

I won't afflict you with the subsequent details of my C.V., which are boring even to me. Suffice it to say that I experienced some degree of "success" in my thirties, almost all of it due to poems I'd written in my twenties, and while those years did feature a fun and dizzying burst of acclaim & minor awards & tweedy/boozy hoopla—I remember thinking *This is it, the Byronic jackpot* when a pair of lithe & giggly female grad students showed up unannounced at my door one night, bearing a fifth of vodka and a book of poems they wanted me to sign—it all quickly fizzled out. One of the girls awarded me an unsolicited handjob but her manner was so clinically lackluster—I felt as if I was having a pimple squeezed—that I stopped her partway through, complaining of a stomachache. When she inquired if it might be gas the night sunk that much further. I milked my brief limelight for what I could—fellowships, grants, community-college readings—but, as I was unable to sustain the momentum (i.e., having bankrupted my cache of youthful poems), my sell-by date soon passed. "I have seen the moment of my greatness flicker," Eliot wrote, and, oh Tom, I know the sight. I don't want to draw the line too rigidly here, or assign sentimental blame, but the fact remains: All the "success" that I had stemmed from the fevered work of my twenties, from the poems I wrote pre-Stellas. By the time anyone noticed the fire, it had already burned down to ashes. Despite my sweaty efforts, I was never again able to match the tone & quality of those early, fumbling, greasy, howl-at-the-moon poems. I was a confessional poet who no longer wanted to confess. Sometimes, when I read my work in public, I felt like a stand-in—an acquaintance presenting the works of a deceased poet, like Kenneth Koch at Frank O'Hara's memorial service reading O'Hara's grand, sweet poem about talking to the sun. "This was the work of a great poet," Koch told the crowd. Immodest words to that effect would run through my head as I read: *This is the work of a great poet. Such a shame that he's gone.* A few hours later would find me plastered at some professorial cocktail party, saying *pbbbbt* when anyone would ask what I was currently working on. After a while only the misfit male grad students fell for my drunk poet routine but they're easy marks anyway. They'd feed me vodka till five A.M., hoping for a tragic Dylan Thomas moment—a pickling they could eulogize.

I went to Poland in 1989, in those heady months when the Iron Curtain was being drawn back from Europe. It was a poet's exchange program for which Alojzy nominated me, and, typifying their history, the Poles got the short end of the stick: me. On second thought, though—scratch that. I've been far too glib already. My time in Poland deserves better. I was supposed to stay for five months but squeezed out more than a year, and even now my memories of it blend and blur: blissfully late late nights in Krakow's candlelit cellar barrooms, drinking bison-grass vodka and chainsmoking those awful Mocne cigarettes and talking capital-A Art with students and poets and on-the-brink novelists and with my omnipresent friend Grzegorz, a crazed, Santa-bearded Crakovian sculptor who disturbingly worked in the nude—all of them contagiously fizzing, crackling, bursting with newly unleashed ambitions—in short, late nights of talking ideas with people for whom words & ideas *mattered*, who had been held captive for so many long years by a single well-intentioned but awful idea, who believed in ideas because their every waking moment thus far in life had been shackled to a bad one and who were now casting about, freely & deliriously, for a new idea, for one that would lift them from the ruck of their history. Down in those cellars I witnessed warmhearted fistfights and boozy, table-pounding declarations and long-private daydreams being traded like baseball cards. For Jan, a poet jaded by what he called the "incompetence" of art in Poland, the dream was to write like a swarm of wasps: finally, that is, to sting. A young philosophy student—Pawel, I think was his name—wanted to open a French restaurant, though he had never tasted French cuisine outside Proust. Grzegorz, on the other hand, longed to someday leave a yellow rose at the Dakota apartment where John Lennon was murdered, and, while he was in New York, to "fuck a powerful Negress."

And then, also, the long sweet quietudes: the hours of those gray-drizzled or snow-muffled mornings that I devoted to learning my father's language, speaking aloud to myself in my seedy little apartment on the lovably foul Ulica Czysta (which translates, inappropriately, to Clean Street) and with my elderly, pince-nez-wearing tutor, Albert; and to rummaging through Poland's literature like a mad pirate sinking his arms elbows-deep into treasure, ransacking the Jagiellonian library so thoroughly that even the night watchmen knew me by name. Polish lit is often derided as hermetic, too history-steeped and insular, but I suspect being raised in the South immunized me to this. It seemed natural to me for literature to obsess over defeats and the long fingers of the past. (I was partial to lost causes even before I became one.) As for my *ex officio* duties, I wrote madly, like the tousle-headed writers depicted in movies tossing pages over their shoulders, and while the poems seemed gorgeous and muse-kissed at the time, it was all, I saw later, well-intentioned dreck—the moment & themes were too big for me. I wrote one poem about some children I saw applauding the arrival of housepainters at an unidentified building; at that hinge of history, in this paint-peeling city, even housepainters bore a messianic glow. Yet the poem, like an unfocused photograph, failed to capture the true pith of it all. Maybe all poems fail in that way. An ode to Venus can hardly rival the sensations of Venus's skin against yours, the press of her naked thigh on yours. It's all secondhand. Black dots on paper that are so intrinsically uninteresting that even a bored dog can't be cajoled into sniffing them.

I'd be remiss, though, if in presenting this slideshow of Poland I neglected to mention poor Margaret. ("Poor Margaret": This is how she's titled in my mental Rolodex, saddled with that adjectival goiter.) She was technically my first wife since Stella and I never officially tied the knot. (We were too cool for that.) I married Margaret on the basis of a single one-night stand and a subsequent torrent of letters: an inadvisable courtship, to be sure. We met at a cocktail reception for foreign arttypes at the residence of some communist bureaucrat—a subminister of *kultury* or somesuch. A fat man with the pinched red face of an infant and such a stink to his breath that you could smell his laughter from across a crowded room. He was also unbearably pompous which was why, aside from the limitless vodka that kept floating my way, I found myself wandering his house secretly tucking meatball canapés into various drawers and cabinets. A decidedly undiplomatic gesture, I know, but the image of that overripe baby sniffing sourly through his house, a few days hence, amused me to no end.

It was Margaret who caught me. She was an art historian

visiting from Connecticut, ten years my senior, a bit thick in the haunches but attractive in a wallflower way. I found her round little eyeglasses fetching, and too her easy, salty laughter. Also that she thought my meatball-sabotaging charming. She said she had a soft spot for "rogues" which made me wince because I'd never heard anyone say that word sincerely aloud. "Well shiver me timbers," I responded, insincerely. Except that she did, in fact, sincerely shiver my timbers a few hours later, when we ended up back at my apartment shredding one another's clothes. I was about to write "like teens in a basement" but then it occurred to me that, despite their hormones, teens rarely do that. It's middle-aged people, desperate to crank up the volume on their fading lives, who do that. In any case she actually ripped my shirt open, the airborne buttons going *ping* against the walls. Once we were in bed she paused to confess, meekly but not primly, that it had been "a long time" since she'd been with a man. I brought her face close to mine and told her, "It's okay. I've never even *been* with a man." Most likely I cadged that from a movie but so what? She laughed that salty laugh and thereafter things went wonderfully, sleeplessly haywire. She was so vocal that when my landlord, an elderly widower, encountered me in the street the next morning, after I'd taken Margaret to the station to catch a train to Warsaw, he dropped his loaf of bread to applaud. Grounds for a marriage? Survey says: X. I'll skip the rest of the story, an epistolary tale for the most part. The marriage was so brief that I think I used the same bath towel for its entire duration.

All of which is a long and perhaps overrevealing roadmap of how I went from poet to translator. My first translations were favors for the pals I'd made in Krakow: exercises in friendship, more or less. It was sweetly satisfying, however, to place their poems in American journals—and in a way that I'd never felt when publishing my own work, I felt *generous* to the audience, as if I was bequeathing something of value to them, rather than, as I felt with my poems, coughing something on them. What's more, I felt freed from the minefields of my own authorial persona; in my translating I aspired to invisibility, and invisibility felt like emancipation. I also found, somewhat to my surprise, that I actually savored the work, was tickled by the process: I *enjoyed* untying all the Gordian knots, piecing together the lingual puzzles, dressing and redressing the words & phrases in my own native garb. And, too, there was something liberating about the imperfection built into the craft. The act of translation is one of approximation. A translation can approach the art in its source language but never quite touch it; close proximity is all, the nearness of its hot breath. As a translator, I could never hope to clone, say, the rose that is a poem—my work could only yield, to paraphrase Nabokov, a thorny cousin to the rose. "What a translator tries for," the great John Ciardi wrote back in the '60s, "is no more than the best possible failure." For someone who'd made a life's habit of failing, this sentiment held a balmy appeal. *The best possible failure.* By the time I started translating, it was all the epitaph for which I could hope. Fail, fail again. Fail better. Am I failing now? Yeah, silly question. Go ahead, you bastards, laugh all you want.

ON THAT NOTE, dear American Airlines, let's check in with Walenty. But let me warn you: My friend Alojzy has engineered a plot twist that I'm not sure I can fully swallow. The *pensione* to which the Bear—now a capitalized bear, for whatever reason, a full-blown *Niedźwiedź*—delivered Walenty turns out to have been the family home of the waitress from the train station café. Small world, no? And the beastly, old-looking, loogie-lobbing woman who runs the joint? Alas, that's her mama. This strikes me as too facile a coincidence—I mean, why have Walenty encounter the girl (whose name is Francesca, FYI, though nicknamed Franca) at the train station at all? Why not have introduced her the following morning, at breakfast—with the same cup of coffee and the same dreamy exchange? My vague guess is that Alojzy might be trying to suggest a kind of lining up of the stars (in Walenty's head, that is), invoking a sense of fatedness. Seems like a misstep to me, however. If at first the plot evoked—albeit faintly, and with much more somber intent—the early parts of Nabokov's *Pnin* (although, on second thought, the louder echo is of Antal Szerb's *Journey by Moonlight*), now it's channeling Spanish-language soap operas. *¿Es su mama?! ¡Ay dos mio!* But then again I abandoned my belief in fate or anything invisible years ago. It wasn't fate, after all, that caused a businessman in Long Island, driving home from the train station (this was in the news a few weeks back), to crash head-on into a car being driven by his teenaged son. It was the two fishbowl-sized martinis he drank after work plus the tall-boy Budweiser he downed on the train.

Regardless, it's Alojzy's damn book. I just untangle the consonants. Here goes:

> She was worried that he would tire but he insisted he was fine; he wanted to walk, he told her, to walk and to walk and to walk. And so they did, into the old *città vecchia* and up the steep ascending lanes, past fish markets and confectionaries and cramped, airless little bookshops and shops selling lampshades and linens and others selling sausages and dried mushrooms and the roasted coffee beans that perfumed the narrow streets. The pockmarks of sniper bullets freckled some of the buildings and there were rows of empty, shuttered shops that must have been owned by Trieste's Jews before the Germans had vanished them; Walenty turned away from these sights, however, refusing to admit them, locking them out. In these moments his pace quickened and Franca confusedly struggled to follow. They did not speak of the past, and often, like elderly couples, they didn't speak at all. They finished at the waterfront where, sitting on the quay,

they shared a local variety of cake that Franca called *pres-nitz* and watched the Adriatic in its implacable blue stillness. Across the bay were terraced vineyards and a white castle and nearby an old man in a cotton suit was transferring the scene onto the canvas propped upon his easel. His lips were moving constantly and it appeared he was conversing with his colors. Walenty noticed the absence of flags on the flag-poles which momentarily swelled his heart. He asked aloud, "Where am I?" Taking his hand in hers, Franca smiled and called him foolish. "You are in Trieste," she said.

A perfect ending, you might think. Cue an accordion *serenata* and the closing credits ("The text in this book was set in Liv-ingstone, the only typeface designed by . . ."). Except, of course, that it's not the end. It never is.

- - - -

OKAY, QUENEAU. Here's a true story and it's not about food. It's about Willa Desforge and Henryk Gniech, the Fords of Annunciation Street, and their befuddled, reclusive little son Benjamin, and maybe it's about love and maybe it's not but then who am I to say? I'm just a mordantly sober guy in an air-port trying to avoid staring at his broken shoelace.

The year was 1963. I was nine years old and mere days away from being ten, and was preoccupied that week, as I had been for months, with two issues: the horse I desperately wanted for my birthday, and the threat of nuclear annihilation. The horse was any black-and-white paint horse similar to the kind ridden by Michael Landon's Little Joe on *Bonanza*. That particular horse was named Cochise though Little Joe more commonly called it "Cooch." ("Cooch," I might note, was Stella's code-word for her genitalia, which, while nicely circular, obviously made dirty talk an impossible exercise in nostalgia for me.) Cochise drank water out of Little Joe's hat and Little Joe also once shared his coffee with Cochise which I thought splendid. A coffee-drinking horse! Perfect for New Orleans—I presumed my horse would fancy our local chicory blend. Naturally I was too young to understand zoning laws and the spatial requirements of livestock but I felt certain my own Cooch would like our backyard just fine and would enjoy being ridden to and from school where I could tie him to the bike rack so long as I left him a bucket of water or a tall *café au lait.* My father barely acknowledged the idea—"Ah . . . no"—while Miss Willa seemed vulnerably noncommittal. "Horses attract flies," she said, but that struck me as a manageable objection. I would blitz the backyard with a thousand sticky flystrips that would twist in the breeze like Tibetan prayer flags. I would keep a flyswatter holstered at all times, and my friend Harry Becker, who lived down the street, promised to do the same for little or no charge. Together, we would make sure the flies weren't a problem.

There was nothing I could do, however, about nuclear death, which I felt certain was close at hand. Its looming shadow, in fact, was my unspoken rejoinder to my mother's other demurral—that perhaps I wasn't old enough for the responsibilities of a horse. *But I'm as old as I'm ever going to be,* went my thinking, what with nuclear winter blowing in soon. I felt its irradiant imminence every time we crawled under our schooldesks when the air-raid siren blew, my eyelids pressed against my left forearm, my other forearm shielding the back of my head, my jutting rump nevertheless fully exposed to the blast wave (that's how America's children would perish, ass-first)—and me wondering all the while whether I would see the fatal flash of light through the shield of my eyelids plus arm & if I would actually feel my hair burning which frightened me slightly more than death (on count two, the nuns said no). I felt that imminence, too, whenever *Bonanza* was interrupted by that dread test of the Emergency Broadcast System and the room temperature seemed to instantly drop by ten degrees. Is that how it would end? From Lorne Greene to a long chilly beep to the thundering Armageddon? "Had this been an actual emergency, you would have been instructed to tune in to your local radio station." I pictured myself running to the cabinet-sized radio/record player in the dining room and furiously dialing in WTIX-AM ("Fun-lovin' WTIX, the Mighty 690!") and listening to the end of the world surfing in on a commercial for Rex Root Beer or that Ponchartrain Beach jingle: *At the beach, at the beach, at Ponchartrain Beach; you'll have fun, you'll have fun, every day of the week.* "Come ride the Scrambler and the Flying Coaster and see the sixteen lively French poodles on the Poodle Expre—" Ka-boom! Come see the giant orange mushroom cloud! The end of everything, you, me, & sixteen lively poodles included! Because of its status as a port city ("a *crucial* port city," the nuns said), New Orleans would be obliterated in the first wave of attacks; this, we were told, was the price we had to pay for living in such an important town. Also it was rumored that the Russians hated Mardi Gras and/or for that matter all parades of a festive nature.

Owing to this fear of mine, which caused even innocuous events like the sighting of a falling star to mutate into moments of fear & trembling (was that a missile?), my father and I tended to divvy up sections of the morning paper in an unorthodox way. The front page went to me and the comics went to him. (Neither of us ever had much use for the sports pages.) I would comb the headlines for clues of our impending doom—the Cuba problem was still sizzling that spring—while my father read the comics wearing *precisely* the same studious expression as me. If the state of the world confounded me, the state of American humor confounded him even more. Perhaps Lucy stealing the football away from Charlie Brown too closely mirrored Polish history to be funny, I don't know. Surely he found Andy Capp's dialect indecipherable (I did too). But then you need to understand that reading the comics wasn't leisure for him: My mother was constantly bemoaning his humorlessness, and he wanted to please her. For him, this was study—a concerted effort to break the code of funny, and perhaps make her laugh. Dagwood Bumstead was his Cyrano, his tutor in romance.

After a while we would trade sections and there would be no sound save the clinking of our spoons and the slurping of mushy cornflakes. I always started with the *Family Circus* which, however corny, tended to soothe & console me. I felt a kind of voyeuristic delight in viewing, through the keyhole that its round border evoked, the quiescent hijinks of a "normal" family—Jeffy's cute-isms, the dopey antics of Barfy the Dog, the dad's frazzled cheeriness. I read somewhere once that scholars had concluded that the cave paintings at Lascaux etc. do not, as previously thought, depict actual events, or animals that the painters had actually seen—what they portray, instead, are animals the painters *wanted* to see, events they *wished* had happened. Is it overreaching to suggest an aesthetic link between prehistoric cave drawings and Bil Keane's *Family Circus?* The kid munching cornflakes says no. The *Family Circus* was my fatty mammoth, my glimpse of the idyll.

Anyway, 1963. It was a Friday, I remember. My birthday was coming on Monday. Finished with the comics & cornflakes, I asked my father about my horse. The backyard had not been properly prepared and I was worried about the work still needing to be done. Transforming a garage into a stable seemed like no minor feat. Would there be time?

"You cannot have no horse in New Orleans," he said.

"There are horses at the fairgrounds," I said.

"Those are racing horses."

"My horse can race. He'll be fast."

"You cannot have no horse in New Orleans," he repeated.

On most mornings Miss Willa tended to sleep in, leaving my father and me to outfit ourselves for work & school, so

I was mildly surprised that morning when she breezed sing-songy into the kitchen. Not entirely surprised, though, since she'd been on one of her blissful streaks lately—what I would later come to understand as "manic episodes." She'd returned to her painting and she'd enrolled in a flower-arranging class; the result was a house overgrown with dried cattails, golden-rod, celosia, purple flax, pepperberries, statice, baby's breath. Every corner was spiked with parched flora. Three magnolia wreaths overlooked the upstairs toilet alone and even my bed-room had been invaded—by bushels of French lavender that perfumed the room so strongly that I reversed the box fan in my room to blow *out* the window.

My father always left for work fifteen minutes before I left for school, which was when I'd sneak in some television. On this day, however, after he left, my mother sat down at the ta-ble with me.

"Benjamin," she said. "Would you like to skip school to-day?"

Even then I was savvy enough to be suspicious. "Why?"

"*Why?* What kind of answer is that?" She sounded a mock harrumph. "Well, I was thinking we might should look at some horses."

You can imagine the detonation of my glee, the way it blew apart my reservations—and, too, my volley of sputtered yes-yes-yesses. My own Cooch! Hot diggety it was happening. The horsemen of the apocalypse would not find me without a steed. I made for the door but she stopped me.

"We'll need to pack you some clothes," she said. "And go pick out some books and toys you'll want to take along."

Naturally I was thrown off by these comments but the last thing I wanted to do was to splash the opportunity with cold questions. I should note that she'd skipped off with me be-fore: twice to Florida, once to New York (we got as far as At-lanta). But children are inherently optimistic, and, of course,

brimming with greed. To employ a horsy metaphor: I purpose-
fully donned blinders as I packed up random belongings and
hauled my suitcase to the garage and into the backseat of our
three-year-old Ford Fairlane. I knew enough to fear my mother's plans and potential delusions but if they yielded me a horse
like Cochise, so be it. Eyes on the prize, baby. Hi-ho Silver. I
must have waited in the front seat for more than an hour—
fiddling with the glove compartment, rolling the window up
and down, chewing the corners off my fingernails. Every so often my mother would load something else into the trunk and
happily promise "one more minute." While I tried to stay sanguine about it all I'll admit my heart dropped an inch or so
when I saw her stuffing all those dried flowers into the trunk
along with her easel and her collected works on canvas. Clearly
we were doing something more than driving to Jefferson Par-
ish to scout horses. The trunk wouldn't close so she tied it with
kitchen twine.

"There," she said, sliding behind the wheel. "Are you
ready?"

"Where are we going?"

The car was rolling out of the garage when she said, "New
Mexico."

For the most part I processed this in silence, until we were
well outside New Orleans and following Highway 61 on its
straight-arrow course toward Baton Rouge. Miss Willa had the
peculiar and discomfiting habit of speaking to me as if I were
a contemporary, and she chatted and chattered as we passed
through those little swamptowns: about Mrs. Marge next door
whose husband was in debt to some gangsters; about Char-
lotte Deviney who was in the hospital for reasons relating to
her "uterus" which for all I knew was the technical term for a
unicorn's horn; but mostly about the painter Georgia O'Keeffe
who I soon gathered was the inspiration for our journey. According to my mother, O'Keeffe had carved herself the per-

fect artist's existence in New Mexico, a place she (and thus my mother) called "the Faraway." New Mexico was stark and haunting and blessed "with the most amazing light," as opposed to Louisiana where, she claimed, there was "no sky." This was baffling to me: What was all that blue in the windshield? Our native landscapes, she told me, were visually impenetrable—nebulous monochromes of moss and muck, devoid of angles and color and light. "Look at it out there," she said. "It's mud. We live in mud. How can you paint mud? How can you live in mud?" In "the Faraway," she said, it was different. Dawn's light dousing the desert was a miracle that would squeeze tears of awestruck joy from our eyes. The sun there was close enough to touch with a fingertip.

I spied a roadside fortuneteller—Highway 61 used to be rife with those—and begged her to stop. "That's ridiculous, Benjamin," she said. (I've never been Bennie to her, always Benjamin—and, I should note, to her alone.) "Those people are charlatans and anyway darling we don't need our fortunes told. We know exactly what lies ahead for us. Things are going to be different for you and me. They're going to be better."

"What about Dad?" I finally asked.

She sighed: Oh, him. There was a silence while her arms tensed against the steering wheel. "Do you love your father, Benjamin?" she asked.

Did I? The question had never occurred to me before. Of course I did. Was it possible not to? He was my father. He poured my cornflakes and shared the paper with me and at night spoke crazywords to me that I clung to like bobbing liferafts. "Yes," I told her.

She sighed again and fetched a Salem from her purse. Publicly, Miss Willa was always quitting smoking, or about to be quitting. She'd announce to us that she was done with cigarettes but then immediately retreat to the bathroom to sneak one. We were always finding filters floating in the toilet bowl, trailed by a tea-colored stain. "Willa!" my father would say. "Someone's cigarette has floated up from the sewers again! We must call plumber."

"Your father is a good man," she said, cracking the window to draft off her smoke. "He is. He's a gentle man. I'll give him that—he wouldn't harm a fly. But he doesn't understand people like you and me. He doesn't want the same things we want. He wants food on the table and a job to go to and he doesn't care what the food tastes like or what the job is. Do you know he's never asked for a raise from Mr. Prejean? Never. He's just too different from you and me. Maybe it's what he went through during the war—that was a hard time, you know."

She took a contemplative drag on the Salem. "He just wouldn't understand the Faraway," she said. "You can have horses there and I can paint. As many horses as you like. That's the life we were meant for, Benjamin. That's what we're headed for."

It was brutally cunning, I realized later: By weaving my desires into hers, by brushing my horses onto her chimeric landscape, she made me an accomplice. Why were we abandoning my father? Because he refused me a horse. Because he was different from us. For one hundred miles she belabored the point: A boy needed wide-open spaces; a woman needed freedom and romance and *life*; the two of us were sun-craving flowers planted in the damp shade; "your father" wouldn't miss us, would barely notice our absence; she'd left him dinner in the icebox plus there were leftover porkchops; God bless the Faraway, Benjamin; the Faraway is our destiny. A thousand LIVE CRAWFISH signs whizzed past. Tourist courts with algae-scummed swimming pools. Spring cotton fields fuzzed with tender green growth that you could only see from certain angles. Crushed, buzzard-picked armadillos that went *unk* beneath our tires. Skinny black kids playing too close to the road, stilled by our passing; for a few inscrutable seconds their hard stares would meet mine as my mother gassed us westward.

Outside Opelousas we stopped for gas and lunch. I remember I ordered *boudin* sausage which repulsed her. "I think there's pig's blood in those," she warned. "Anyway it's not a good idea to trust the food outside New Orleans." She let me buy bubblegum cigarettes and I chainsmoked them into Texas, my window cracked to exhaust the powdered-sugar smoke. I thought twice about ditching the gum out the window, wondering if such discarded sweets were what lured doomed armadillos onto the highway. So instead I gobbed the spent pieces together with my hands and wrapped them in newspaper. By Huntsville I had a baseball-sized wad.

"Is New Mexico important?" I asked her.

"Important?" she said. "To us? I think it's terribly important."

"No," I said. "To the Russians. Do they think it's important?"

"I don't know what you mean."

"Well, New Orleans is important because it's a port city and that's why the Russians are going to bomb it. Are they going to bomb New Mexico, too?"

"Oh, honey, no. Where do you get all this? You don't need to be afraid. The Russians wouldn't bomb New Mexico. It's too beautiful and there's no one there anyway. You won't need to worry anymore."

I found this information hard to digest—and weirdly disappointing, too. For all my nightsweats about nuclear attack, there was something mesmerizing and exciting about it as well, something that felt the way a dangerous bout of lust would strike me later in life—an amalgam of dread and desire that made my heart race, that injected my veins with the sizzle of doom. I *wanted* to worry about it.

We ate dinner at an Old West–themed restaurant where the waiter wore a cowboy hat and a string tie and called me pad-nah. "You see, honey?" my mother said. "We're in the West now. It's different." She suggested I order sarsaparilla which she claimed was the soda of choice for cowboys but it tasted just like root beer to me. When the jukebox played Marty Robbins's "El Paso" my mother sang along until I begged her to stop. Her church-pew soprano on "wild as the west Texas *wi-ihhhhhh-nnnnn-d*" was drawing stares. "Oh, don't be so serious," she said. "For heaven's sake, you're just like your father sometimes." To keep myself occupied I drew a sloppy crayon portrait of the waiter on the back of the kids' menu. "Oh, how wonderful," my mother said. "Let me show him." I protested, lividly, but she showed him anyway. "Ain't that some'n, pad-nah," he said with an unmistakable air of bullshit. "My son is very talented," my mother said, clasping my hand. When the waiter was out of earshot she asked me if I didn't think he was handsome. I shrugged.

"Oh, you don't know, you're a *boy*," she said. After glancing at the nearby tables, she leaned in toward me, speaking as softly as a wartime confidante. "Benjamin," she said. "Let me ask you something. Would it bother you if there was a new man around?"

"What kind of man?"

"Not so loud. Just someone to take your mother dancing once in a while. And maybe to play with you. Throw a ball, that sort of thing. Why, maybe a man who knows something about horses."

"I don't know."

"But it wouldn't bother you?"

We spent the night in a cabin-court room at a motel my mother chose because of the huge white steer horns that crowned its roadside sign. "How fun," she said. The blankets on the beds were decorated with the same horns. There was a black-and-white TV in the room but the antenna was broken and it didn't get any channels, so I dipped into the Gideon Bible I discovered in the drawer of the nightstand between our beds. Midway through the Book of Revelation—I've always started books at the end—my mother ordered me to turn off the light. After that I lay awake listening to the purr of highway traffic and watching the glow from passing headlights roam the walls of our room. "This is nice, isn't it?" my mother said to the dark. It wasn't obvious she was talking to me. "Goodnight," is what I said back. "Yes," she went on. "It's good that it's nice."

- - - -

PARDON THE INTERRUPTION but guess who was just here? The Munchkin! (Cribbing from Alojzy, and his upgrade from *niedźwiedź* to *Niedźwiedź*, I have promoted her from munchkin to Munchkin.) Surely you remember: the one with the handheld slot machine and the comatose husband and that packet of Kleenex currently tucked in my satchel. I was "scribbling away" (to use Oshkosh Bob's phrase) at the above, adrift in my own mental Texas, when I felt a finger jabbing me in the chest. Rather hard, too: a barfight-quality poke. "Hey, buster," she said to me, flashing a bridgeworked smile. "I was heading out for some air and saw you sitting here."

"I could use some air myself," I told her.

As we walked through the terminal she asked me, "Have they told you when you're getting out of here?"

"By April, guaranteed," I said.

"Holy moly," she said. "You're joking."

"I am."

"Well," said she, "anything is possible."

Out on the sidewalk I lit her cigarette for her. "Oh goody, a gentleman," she said. Then, holding the lit cigarette away from her, examining it with distaste, the way Stella used to sometimes appraise me in the mornings, she said, "These darn things. I went twenty-two years without. And then I got the call from the state police, saying Ralph had been in the crash. I didn't even make it to the hospital before stopping to buy a pack. I had to pick my jaw up off the floor when they told me the price. I think they were sixty-five cents back when I quit the first time. Darn things."

"They keep my hands occupied," I said. "Otherwise I might strangle myself."

"Now I know you're joking," she said.

I was. But anything is possible.

She'd been to Vermont to visit her daughter and grandchild. Her daughter was married to a high-strung political aide who, while smart, worked "for a Socialist." Her granddaughter was two, she told me, and while otherwise angelic, had "sleep problems." ("Sleep *issues*, I mean," she corrected herself, having obviously been corrected herself.) The parents thought it best to let the girl "cry it out" so after putting her down in her crib they inserted earplugs and pretended to read magazines downstairs while grinding their teeth between spurts of bickering. From the first night, Granny Munchkin found the little girl's shrieking unendurable, and so planted herself cribside, humming lullabies to her. It didn't work, she told me, but it was *something*. A psychiatrist might have noted the parallels between this and her longrunning vigil at her husband's bedside, but I am not a psychiatrist. I am a smoker. I noted that it must have been nice to see her daughter.

"Oh of course," she said, shrugging lightly as if to conceal a dinge of sadness. "We go back and forth sometimes, about Ralph. She thinks it's time for us to let him go. I don't think that's up to us. Who am I to say what's hopeless and what's not? Leave it to the angels."

She asked if I had children. "A daughter," I said, shrugging lightly myself. I gave her the skinniest skinny about that: Speck getting married tomorrow, me trying to get there. The single-sentence summary to which this letter and maybe my life is one long blazing footnote. The conversation moved on, nostalgically, smokily, to the good old days of air travel—the regulation era, with its red-eye flights and goopy-but-satiating meals and dapperly dressed travelers and (here comes my two cents) svelte and allegedly immoral stewardesses and rear-of-the-aircraft smoking sections—and then the Munchkin said *What the heck* and slid another cigarette from her pack. After I'd lit it she extended a hand to me and said, "Margaret."

"Bennie," I said, pumping her plump hand. "Margaret? I was married to a Margaret once." Ha ha, me. Always playing the rogue. Cue a jellybowl laugh from Ed McMahon.

"Well, I hope you were good to her," she said, with what looked like a wink but might also have been a stigmatic tic.

Whoops. How to respond to that one? I stared for a moment, blinking, watching a baggage porter gnaw a fingernail while leaning against his empty cart. I thought I was good. Tried to be. Damn we were lonely people, the two of us. The day after our berserk tryst in my apartment I received a telegram from Margaret in Warsaw: MORE, SHE SAYS, MORE. Who could fail to grin wolfishly after opening that one? Later that night I composed a slapdash poem for her about our night together, as seen from the perspective of one of my sacrificial shirt-buttons. To be honest I didn't remember all that much of the evening—my blackouts were never fully black, more like burning charcoal: some parts black, some parts gray, some parts orange and blistering—but I recalled enough fleshy details for the purposes of light verse.

The letter she wrote back was so deliciously smutty (as opposed to my cutesy Donne-ish ditty) that I felt I should be charged by the minute for reading it. And then rereading it, whew. Before I had time to respond I received another letter from her, this one winsome and chatty and more but not exclusively concerned with matters above-the-waist. Much of it was about the nineteenth-century painter whose work she was in Poland studying (Henryk Rodakowski) and how I resembled one of his subjects—minus, that is, his rabbinical beard, pear-shaped physique, bulbous copper nose, and obvious blighted penury. The eyes, she said. Something about those starving-hound eyes. (Woof, I said to the letter.) She'd made a rubbing of Rodakowski's tombstone while in Krakow, and enclosed a copy of it for me—an adolescent gesture, to be sure, like your college girlfriend sending you a rubbing of Jim Morrison's grave from Paris, but then perhaps it was an adolescent affair all around. An end-of-summer-camp romance. Or no, scratch that: rather two middle-aged sadsacks fumbling loosely in the dark, pretending they could start fresh. Pretending that springy bed with the parchment-colored sheets was the backseat of an Oldsmobile parked by the lake, pretending the steamy odor of vodka on my rottening skin was the smell of 75¢/gallon gasoline or a horny teenaged boy's drugstore cologne.

Forgive me: I've ladled too many memories into your bowl already. But allow me one more spoonful. (Your better alternative is to put me on a plane but I can see that's too much to ask.) I haven't thought about poor Margaret in more than a decade, meaning never sober. And now comes Margaret the Munchkin, High Commandant of the Margarets Brigade, wanting to ascertain that I was good to her sister-in-Margarethood. Well, define good. I've been trying for years, lady, without success or even noticeable progress, like some pinhead into his third decade of trying to outwit a Rubik's Cube.

We continued our correspondence even after she returned to the states, Margaret and I. If we weren't writing daily, then almost daily. How I loved those letters! With each one she became something new in my mind, transformed and retransformed in my squiffed imagination. When I was feeling shallow & thick-witted, I would read her letters about Rodakowski and her work, as well as her responses to my old poems (which she poignantly tracked down via an out-of-print-book search), marveling at her incisiveness and feeling somehow wiser by my association, by the fact that I had made her shriek those voluptuous arias in my bed and then telegram me their echoes the next day. In my lonesome unloved hours I would read her saucier letters, lowering myself into the hot bath of her affection, blood rushing to the center of my body. In the funhouse of my mind my images of her—scarce and scattered to begin with—grew bent and warped. Who was this woman? Did the trail of freckles between her breasts that I remembered, those caramel droplets of sunlight that I kept following in daydreams, truly belong to her? Or were they some other woman's, or no other woman's? I had only her continuous stream of letters and my dim memories of that night which seemed ever less trustworthy as the weeks passed. Admittedly, I draped her in hopes. Here might be a woman who could save me, I thought, who could rescue me from myself. The old drunk's fantasy. Or maybe: Here was a woman I could love. Raptly, I began envisioning our life together: me writing beside a fire in some log-chinked, Frostian Connecticut farmhouse (she'd written to me about the farmhouse, though the chinked logs were my imagined detail), sipping but not guzzling brandy (my naive ambition was never to quit drinking, only to moderate it), some Anglo-Saxon breed of dog snoring at my feet, big marshmallow snowdrifts visible through an ice-latticed window; her drinking muted blends of tea in another room, studying Rodakowski's fat-nosed portraits until that lush desire—which was primarily what I knew of her, firsthand anyway—overcame her, with the force of a popped champagne cork, at which point she would sashay into my room and straddle my chair and et cetera et cetera until even the fire would be blushing. Rinse and repeat. I cherished the thought, as they say. Maybe being in Poland at the time contributed something to my imaginative fervor: Everyone around me was dreaming big. Everything seemed possible. Moreover, I wasn't me over there, or at least didn't feel the soggy old weight of being me. Perhaps, courtesy of Margaret, I could prolong not being me—especially since my Polish visa was set to expire. My letters grew increasingly fictional, in spirit rather than statement; I wanted, desperately, to enact this delusive life I'd cooked up, and needed to sell her on it.

After two and a half months I proposed marriage. By letter, of course. This was after an especially rotten night of drinking during which I'd been roughed up by some students, after Grzegorz abandoned me at a party to which he'd earlier dragged me. I was the only one there over twenty-five and apparently my benign two A.M. flirtation with a sweet little number in counterfeit Levi's irked the boys. I suppose, not without empathy, that they were tired of rich old foreigners trying to bed their women. The Russians had been bad enough; now they had to contend with this tanked American poet, slurring lines from Keats. One of them put me in a full Nelson, hoisting me by my underarms, while another led us out the doorway to the stairs. They hauled me halfway down the stairs before chucking me the rest of the way down. Something—the banister, the vodka, or a combination of both—knocked me unconscious for an hour, maybe two. Suffice it to say that it wasn't a pleasant awakening. We drunks always talk about "hitting bottom" but usually without this much precision. If my soul could have quit my body at that moment, could have stood up and brushed itself off and walked away, leaving that corporeal husk crumpled at the foot of the stairs . . . well, unfortunately I didn't know how to pull off that particular magic trick, so the point is moot. Just before dawn I staggered home, chanting *enough* in every language I knew. As the dawn crept across Krakow I wrote Margaret to ask her to marry me, sealed the envelope, and sucked down some ibuprofen. Then I slept, vampirically, until nightfall.

She called me to respond. This was maybe a week and a

half later. I hadn't remembered the odd squeak in her voice; it sounded as if it stemmed from a mechanical issue, as if some glottal hinge was rusty and perhaps she needed to gargle some WD-40. I asked if she had a cold which she denied. "Must be a bad connection," I said. She accepted my proposal ("yes, she says, yes"), as you already know, and we set about planning a wedding. Or rather she did: She knew an "interfaith minister" who performed weddings in her study. I said it sounded peachy. I was nearly forty years old and I'd never called anything in my life peachy before, not even a peach. This was either a very peachy sign, or a decidedly bad omen.

She picked me up at JFK. Thankfully she was holding a sign —MORE, SHE GETS, MORE; very charming, though the trope was beginning to wear—because I didn't recognize her. In my defense she was wearing a different dress and had gotten her hair severely chopped. Also I'd never noticed she was flat-footed. My fiancée was 4F. She wanted to make out in the airport but, as sweetly as I could, I suggested we move along, and not only because airports strike me as woefully inappropriate venues for passion. Her Connecticut farmhouse was indeed a farmhouse, somewhere underneath its vinyl siding, but the farm had disappeared decades ago. Split-level homes from the '70s surrounded it like architectural weeds. There was a lake nearby, as she'd written, covered with a rind of antifreeze-colored duckweed; an open meadow had formerly separated her house from the lake, but now two houses were under construction there, gagging the neighborhood's last breathable space. She had a paddleboat tied up at the lake, she said. The blue one. She suggested I take a spin.

That's mostly what I did, to be honest: spin. I'd head out to the lake in the mornings, sometimes with the newspaper but usually not, and paddle the blue boat out to the middle of the verdigris lake where I would sit drinking for hours. In no time at all the duckweed would reclaim the glossy black trail of my wake and I would drink myself to a floating stillness. Even the day after our wedding—a short, crisply secular exchange of vows witnessed by Margaret's younger sister and her department chair—found me on the lake, rather than on my new bride. To be frank I was having problems in the bedroom; for whatever reason, my body wasn't much interested in being there. Reaching under the sheets inevitably yielded a defeated sigh from Margaret. She'd pull the covers up over her unfreckled breasts and together, in silence, we'd watch the cracks on the ceiling. Their entertainment value was nil. Every night the same rerun.

Sometimes, when I was out on the paddleboat, I'd see kids fishing from a footbridge at one end of the lake, but I never saw them catch anything. I admired their faith. I watched burgers get grilled, lawns get mowed. One time I saw a guy in denim shorts, having exhausted himself yanking the starter cord of a recalcitrant push-mower, pick the damn thing up and heave it down the lawn toward the lake, then kick it for added measure. Not romantically, this reminded me of the night I'd proposed; why, I'd been that mower. When the guy glanced up and saw me staring, he pointed at the machine as if to assign blame. I gave no response. Sometimes, too, I'd spy Margaret, my new wife, at the edge of the lake, leveling the same stare at me as I'd leveled at the mower thug. Sometimes she'd wave. Sometimes I'd wave back. On occasion she'd leave a picnic lunch, cold lemon chicken or something, the knife and fork tied together with ribbon. The ribbon broke my heart. Oh what the fuck had I done this time.

Margaret ended it. Or rather it was Margaret who spoke the ending aloud. I didn't have the guts. "This is silly," she said matter-of-factly one evening. "You don't love me."

"I want to," I said.

"It doesn't work that way," she said. "It's not a matter of willpower."

We were remarkably sanguine about it. That is to say, she was. I was just me. More than anything else she felt foolish, she said. It had just felt so good to *connect*, she said. The *connecting* felt so good, so strong. Part of her, she admitted, had felt swindled in these final few days, as if she'd fallen for some swarthy con artist's ruse. Yet she'd decided she wasn't the one who'd been duped—I was. I'd conned myself. Weakly, I argued, but it was all for show. After a while she brewed us some coffee and when she delivered me a mug she was unhappily laughing and saying, "Never in a million years did I think I'd end up in a fly-by-night marriage. My oh my. Well, Lorna"—that was her sister—"had you pegged from the get-go. Said you can't base a marriage on a one-night stand. I told her to loosen up. I said you don't turn away love because it doesn't ring the doorbell wearing a suit and carrying roses. Sometimes it comes, I don't know—in through the window."

"Like a mosquito," I said.

"I hate it when she's right."

"We could try counseling," I offered.

"Oh Bennie," she said. "Shut up."

Cut now to the present, or rather to the nearer past.

"No," I answered the Munchkin. "I wasn't so good to her."

She arched her eyebrows. "There's always tomorrow," she said.

"Oh Jesus, I haven't seen her since—"

"To be good," she said. "There's always tomorrow to be good. Now, here," she went on, rummaging through her fanny-pack until that handheld slot machine appeared in her hand. "I've got a cot in there someone's going to steal, so you've got to be quick. But take a spin. Go ahead."

Why not? I depressed the fat oval button at the base. Two bars and a cherry. Close but no cigar, or no cigarette to be more accurate. "One more try," I said.

"That's the only way to win," she said.

Rightly, as it turned out. Three sevens! "Jackpot!" I bellowed. Count 'em, baby! I flashed the machine at the Munchkin and did a giddy little shuffle on the sidewalk. The baggage porter paused from molesting his fingernail to watch me for a moment, and had he not swiftly resumed his chewing I might've tried high-fiving him. Some skin for my win, my brutha! Read 'em and weep. There must be thousands of human beings stranded at this airport but at that odd moment I was the only one dancing. Go figure.

"See?" said the Munchkin. "Nice going, buster."

"What do I get?" I asked her.

"'Get'?" she said, and considered it for a moment. "Well, not money, if that's what you're hoping. You get points."

"Oh," I said, deflating. "What do I get with the points?"

She looked at me as if I was an idiot. "Happiness," is what she said, softly prying the machine from my hand.

- - - -

DEAR AMERICAN AIRLINES, it occurs to me that those whizbang handheld slot machines might be a good investment for you. Here's how it would work: Passengers would be handed one of the machines with their boarding pass. At the gate, thirty minutes prior to the scheduled departure, everyone would have to take a spin at the very same time. If everyone hits jackpot simultaneously, a massive cheer goes up and the plane departs on time. If not, they wait one hour and try again. The upside for you is that we passengers would bemoan our bad luck rather than castigate you. Fate would get the blame, not the poor gate attendants who in this scenario will just shrug and smile and bid us better luck next time. Your planes would take off at about their normal rate but the populist heat would be diverted. See? I offer this idea to you *gratis* though you should feel encouraged to cite me in the press release. It would make my mother so proud to see me in the business pages. In fact, here's my quote: "'Americans love gambling, but their main form of gambling—heading to the airport—has been flagrantly rigged for years,' said Benjamin Ford, a transportation consultant who devised the system for the Texas-based airline. 'The Jackpot Take-Off® from American Airlines is a game of pure chance, and takes the flying game out of corporate hands and delivers it into the hands of the people.'" Tweak as needed, and you're welcome.

Speaking of Texas: I believe that's where I left off with my tale of mother-son adventure, my childhood roadtrip with Sally Paradise. So as they used to say in the western pulps: *Meanwhile, back at the ranch.* I remember Texas lasting forever —my mother asked me to draw a picture of it, so I drew a straight horizontal line and called it quits—but we made it to New Mexico by the second evening. I don't believe my mother had a clear destination in mind, other than New Mexico, i.e. "the Faraway." We drifted north toward Santa Fe, which was near to where O'Keeffe's Ghost Ranch was located, but Miss Willa was jumpy and anxious once we crossed the state line, as if she expected the Faraway to be rapturously self-evident—as if she thought she would recognize one of the abstract landscapes from O'Keeffe's *oeuvre* and then need only to park the car. Suddenly invalidated, the Texaco roadmap we'd been unfolding and folding since New Orleans sank beneath a pile of candy wrappers and other travel-debris on the floorboards. "We're close, Benjamin," she said. "I can feel it." That evening's sunset was characteristically crimson but insufficiently magnificent for her. "It must be too dry," she said. "The air needs a little moisture for a *really* fiery sunset. You'll see."

We were on an ominous desert sideroad after dark, without a single distant lightbulb in sight, when I shrieked. I felt a sudden hot pain on the skin of my ankle—a sharp, scalding stab—and instantly, because we were out west, presumed I'd been bitten by a rattlesnake that had somehow taken up residence in our car. "What?" my mother screamed, flinging an arm over my chest as the Fairlane swerved across the road throwing sideways bursts of gravel. "Snake!" I screamed back, which only increased the swerving; it felt like we were spinning 360s down the road. I skittered up onto the seat and grabbed my stinging ankle which to my befuddled surprise I found wet and hot, as if I'd been attacked by . . . soup. "I'm covered in poison!" I announced, holding up my dripping hand, and as my mother said *Wait wait* and braked the car there was a tremendous explosion from under the hood followed by billows of steam or smoke (we weren't sure which) that came rolling across the windshield. The car spluttered and startled and I was thrown forward onto the floorboards where a blistering liquid rained all over me. When the car came to a standstill at the roadside we leapt out of it in tandem and ran panicked circles around it, in opposite directions, meeting at the front of the car where my mother gathered me into her arms to examine my wound and to issue a cc'd prayer to Jesus, Mary, and Joseph. "Oh, Benjamin, no," she said, which convinced me I was a goner even though the pain was dissipating. "I don't see any bite," my mother said, and brought a wet fingertip to her nose to smell it. She frowned. "I think it's car stuff."

"What kind of car stuff?"

"I don't know. Not gasoline. It smells . . ."

"Like what?"

"Like pee-pee—a little bit. Though sweeter . . ."

"The car peed on me?" I asked.

"Tinkled," she said. "We say 'tinkled.'"

Together, we turned our gaze to the Ford Fairlane. Steam was cascading from beneath the hood, and typhoons of it, smelling weirdly like corn syrup, were engulfing us. My mother stood up and gingerly approached the hood, ready to leap backwards, the way a pup appraises some unfamiliar thing that may or may not be alive and befanged. Meanwhile I walked beyond the rear of the car to assess our location. We were on the side of a two-lane road smack dab in the parched New Mexican nowhere. One of those "blue highways" Americans have taken to romanticizing now that our cars don't break down every four hundred miles. There were no road signs, and not a single car or truck had passed us or was showing distant, glimmering hints of approaching. The silence was downright stunning, if you got far enough away from the engine's hissing demise. No light, no sound, no humidity: the absence of everything. I remember thinking this must be what space was like—the night sky was breathtakingly overfreckled with stars—or the aftermath of Armageddon. Or the Faraway, I thought.

"Your damn father," my mother was muttering when I returned. "He spends all damn day tinkering with foreign cars but doesn't take care of his own cars, excuse my language. But isn't that just like him. Well, I guess he gets the last laugh."

"You said he doesn't laugh."

"It's a figure of speech, Benjamin," she said. "Now what do we do?"

I went to fetch the roadmap but it was soaking in a pool of antifreeze, the source of my scalding. I remembered that the map had cautioned drivers navigating the desert to always carry water in case of emergencies but we'd neglected that advice. For the first time I noticed how cold it was, which surprised me—I'd thought the desert would be hotter than New Orleans. Shivers overwhelmed me.

"I think we should lift the hood," I told my mother.

"You do it," she said.

A hot blast of steam clobbered me, not unpleasantly, as I unlatched and raised the car's hood. We stood for a while watching the roiling steamclouds and listening to the stalled engine rattle and ping until my mother suggested we climb back into the car to stay warm. "You should turn off the lights," I said. "That runs the battery down."

"So you're a mechanic now?" she snapped back. "Did your father teach you that?"

"Everyone knows that."

"Don't you 'everyone' me, Benjamin," she said.

"Well, it's true."

"I suppose you want to grow up to fix cars, is that right?"

"I don't know."

"Maybe you should have stayed back with your father then. The two of you could be greasemonkeys together. Just imagine! You could tinker with jalopies and never wash your hands and fall asleep in front of the damn television set, excuse my language, and eat those miserable pirogues every night for dinner. There's a life."

"Pierogies," I said. "*Pirogues* are boats."

"I know what a *pirogue* is! I misspoke! And you have some nerve correcting me, young man. Honestly. *Pirogues*, pierogies. Your father wouldn't know the difference so long as he had ketchup." She lit a cigarette, smoking it with the ravenous inhalations of a junkie. "Oh for God's sake look where we are. Blast your father anyway."

When a car passed, without stopping or even slowing, my mother said, "There went our chance. There it went. Our last chance."

"I'm cold," I said.

This frail admission seemed to calm or steady her — to pluck some maternal string within her, however untuned. Gently, she said, "I know, honey. I'm cold too. It's our New Orleans blood. We weren't designed for this." She reached over and ran a hand through my hair. "Everything will be okay, I promise."

Roughly a half-hour later the interior of the car filled with a dazzle of white light; a pickup truck had pulled in behind us. We listened to the sputtery growl of its engine, filtered through an injured muffler, and the creak-clank of its doors closing, with our eyes fixed on the car's side-view mirrors for a glimpse of our rescuers. We each had a view: There were two men, approaching our car on both sides. The man on my side was young, somewhere in his twenties, and wearing a straw cowboy hat, bluejeans, and a woolen vest festooned with stripes of blue, purple, and black. The moment his face appeared in the window I could see he was an Indian or what are nowadays called Native Americans—glossy black braids dangled at the sides of his coppery face. When our eyes met he grinned, displaying wet purple gums where his two front teeth ought to have been, and with a knuckle he rapped on the glass.

"Oh my God!" my mother screamed. "*Indians!* Lock the doors, Benjamin, lock them *now!*"

I looked at the man on the other side of my window. "Need help?" he mouthed.

"For the love of dear almighty God I will not be scalped," my mother was saying.

"I think they want to help us," I said.

"They want our *scalps*, Benjamin! They're going to rip our foreheads off!"

The man outside my window—sweetly frowning, hands on his knees—appeared very puzzled. He stood up, looking at his companion across the roof of our car, and shrugged. I raised my index finger to him, to say please wait. He frowned and shrugged again but didn't walk away.

"They want to help us," I told my mother.

Miss Willa's hands were on the steering wheel, tight like a race-car driver's, and I could see her chest heaving. She seemed on the verge of vomiting but in an instant I saw that it was sobs coming, not vomit. Her grip on the wheel tightened even more as tears ran down her face. Her head bobbed up and down as if the tears were too heavy for her neck to support. A croaking sound echoed up from her lungs.

"They aim to kill us," she sputtered. "I saw it in a movie. Oh, Benjamin, what have I done?"

"No, Mother," I said. "Our car needs fixing. I think they want to help."

"Why?" she screamed, and then screamed it again, and then again, banging the steering wheel with the flat of her hands so violently I felt sure the wheel would snap off. "Why does this happen to me? Why can't it ever be the way it should be? Tell me that, why?" In a frenzy she searched the car for something else to hit and for a moment I feared she would slap me. Instead she punched the window with the side of her fist, six or seven times, and each time with an escalating shriek; I saw the Indian on her side jump back.

"Tell them to kill me," she said. "Do it."

"They're not going to kill you."

"What do you know?" She was hissing at me. "You don't know anything. Do you have any idea what it's like to be an animal in a cage? Why in God's name do I even try anymore? You tell me that, Mr. Know-Everything. Tell me! All I wanted was to give you a better life. You! You've ruined me, you and your father. Y'all have sucked the life right out of me. I can't even sleep at night. What's the point of dreaming? There is no point with you two. It's cruel, is all it is. All I wanted was to give you a horse. A stupid damn horse. That's why we're here, Benjamin," she said, and at this she started sobbing again, barely able to make the words, "for your stupid damn horse."

"I don't want a horse anymore," I said. My voice was cracking. "I'm hungry. I just want a cheeseburger."

Maybe it was the word *cheeseburger* that did it: How truly dire can your situation be if the word *cheeseburger* is involved? For what felt like a long time she wept, with her eyes clamped shut, and then she wiped her eyes and inhaled deeply to compose herself and wiped her hands on the pleats of her dress. When she said it was okay I got out of the car and spoke to the Indians who didn't ask about the woman sitting alone inside. Was I thus aware, at that single-digit age, of just how to fetch my mother from her mental Faraway? Did I know, consciously, that appealing to whatever splinter of maternal dutifulness was embedded within her—by lamenting that I was cold, or hungry, or hurt—would sometimes reel her back in? Children are instinctual creatures, wholly capable of strategy. I must have looked pathetic there, a skinny-legged child all but swallowed by the dark passenger seat, begging his mother to put aside her wild, discordant visions—the purple fantasies of idyllic independence and artistic freedom and sexual license clashing with her provincial fears of the unknown, with her numskulled nightmares of cinematic savages carving off her forehead—so that he could fill his small belly with a *cheeseburger*. Acting pitiable was a tack that would serve me well with my mother, as a child, but decidedly not so well with others, as an adult. I remember when Stella smashed me with that glass: I merely sat there, dazed but not entirely so, letting the blood pour down my cheeks and onto my shirt, contorting my face in the noble way of the punchdrunk & bloodsmeared Rocky Balboa when Mickey was begging him, in the ring-corner, to let him stop the fight, and invoking, furthermore, that most poignant detail: that Stella had hit me with our only water glass. As if my sole concern was for our domestic infrastructure—my eyesight be damned. I didn't curse and run to the mirror to flush my wound and pick the shards from my eye. I didn't push her away. I just sat there passively, using the gush of blood to appeal to her sense of pity, which was not so dissimilar to the pose I adopted in my "confessional" poems: that of a child, wounded and confused by life's fangs, pleading for a cheeseburger when all I really wanted was to scream *Stop stop I want out*.

We rode back to town in the Indians' truck. The driver had a kind, jowly face and his round belly was capped with a silver belt buckle the size of a 45-rpm record. The other Indian, the one whose face had appeared in my window, was his nephew, and he was drunk. His eyes resembled the famously red poppies that O'Keeffe was so fond of painting. The uncle had looked at our engine, while my mother sat in the car, and said a lot of automotive gobbledygook that even today I would probably have a difficult time following, though I vaguely remember his diagnosis: a hole in the radiator, a torn-up belt, some grim et ceteras. I asked him if he could fix it and he said no but told me he had a cousin who could—farther down the road, in town. He'd tow it in the morning. There was a "nice motel" in town too; the uncle pointed to his truck and said for us to load up. My mother never said a word to them; every now and then, on the ride to town, a little sob would escape from her and she would cover her mouth as if she'd burped. A preacher on the radio filled the silence for us with the story of a man who lost a finger to a grain thresher but whose prayers caused a new finger to grow from the nub of the old one. When the radio preacher shouted *Hallelujah* the Indians repeated it, even the drunk nephew who blazed through four cans of Coors on the way to town while staring out the black window.

They dropped us off at a motel with an unpaved parking lot and told us where we could find our car the next day. In a more humid and genteel version of her New Orleans accent, my mother called them "saints" and "Samaritans" and pressed into the uncle's hand a dollar bill, which was examined and accepted without comment. I felt I should follow them and say something more, but didn't. My mother's hand was planted on my shoulder while she blithely waved goodbye with her other hand.

I never got my cheeseburger though to be honest I was never that hungry. My mother went into the room, which smelled of antique cooking grease, and resumed weeping while I sat in an aluminum chair outside the door, bundled in a thin wool blanket, minding the activity at the town's single intersection. Those semis sounded like thunder. After a while I went to the front desk and asked the old woman there how to make a long-distance call and she guided me through the protocol of calling collect. It was two A.M. in New Orleans but my father answered on the first ring.

We celebrated my birthday at a diner across the highway from the motel. My mother was in no mood to sing—she didn't have enough money to pay for the motel plus the car repair and was stricken with worry; she didn't know my father was on his way—but the fat waitress and a coffee-slurping trucker beside me serenaded the delivery of a bowl of ice cream in which a forest of ten candles had been planted. "You're a man now," the trucker said to me. "A big ol' man." He pulled a quarter from my ear and let me keep it and also gave me an American Legion baseball cap way too big for my head. My mother made me ask for his address so I could write him a thank-you note. The trucker laughed and said the diner was as close to home as anywhere and the fat waitress confirmed that with a caustic chuckle as she refilled his coffee mug. To me it seemed like a condition to admire.

My father arrived early the next morning—it was still dark. When we opened the door he was standing there holding a present for me, wrapped in the *Times-Picayune*'s Sunday comics pages, a handsome toy horse with moveable legs. At first my mother was angry and accused him of hunting her down like a lost dog. They fought and she locked herself in the bathroom while my father sat on the edge of the bed with his head in his hands. She softened when he paid the motel bill and got the Fairlane out of hock at the repair shop. The plan was for us to follow him back to New Orleans. Outside the diner, after breakfast, my father sat in the Fairlane and revved its engine to assess its durability for the long drive home. "Okay, okay," he kept saying. We stood together beside the car door, my mother & I, me holding my toy horse and her stroking my hair. The air was dusty and filled with the screech-hiss sound of truck brakes and drifting gray puffs of diesel exhaust. The mesas to the west looked nothing like O'Keeffe's landscapes: They were muted and dunnish, bleached by the high late-morning sun, all traces of life burned from their flanks save for a stubble of metallic-looking plantlife. It was what I imagined the world would look like in the aftermath of nuclear war: the tops blown off the mountains, the land stripped of color, the air tinged with a toxic haze. Yet the evocation didn't frighten me. Let the world melt in flames, let it rip my forehead off. Let anything come. "It's good," my father said of the car. "If this needle start to go high, you pull over."

I remember my mother's smile: a half-smile, really, but affectionate, in her way. We'd been through this before: those two times to Florida, when I was too young to remember it all, and that time in Atlanta when my mother's cousin Sylvia placed the call to my father while her husband secretly disabled our car (I learned later) by stealing the distributor cap. She would flee, and my father would inevitably fetch her home. Maybe that was always the point: marriage as an awful game of hide-and-go-seek. Maybe my mother never expected, or even intended, to actually escape. After all she was terrible about not finishing her paintings and her suicide attempts were almost always dramatic half-measures. Standing beside the car in that hot cloud of road dust and tailpipe vapors, her hair tossed by the wind, she smiled at my father and said to him, "I don't know why you always do this."

"I did not know," he replied, with neither tenderness nor bitterness, "that I had choice."

TWO A.M. AT O'HARE. The airport resembles refugee camps I've seen on the evening news except for the more upscale luggage and the Starbucks cups strewn willy-nilly amongst the refugees. People are even curled up atop cardboard boxes. Cardboard boxes! Where did they find appliance-sized boxes in an *airport?* This world never fails to withhold its juicier secrets from me. An hour or so ago they issued a stern last-call for cots which were being distributed at Gate K2. Oh screw it, I figured: The Munchkin deserves cushioning, not me. Let the children sleep while this old coot goes spelunking back through his life, swinging this lamp in a dumb search for truth. So I've staked out a place up here by the ticket counters where it's not quite so crowded and where there's easy access to the nifty sidewalk smoking lounge. I found a seat with a broken chair arm and though I tried to snap the arm off, to widen the seat for the relief of my aggrieved spine, it wouldn't budge. Boy howdy this place is well-armed against comfort.

I should note that your giant neon logo, with its nuzzling A's and that art deco eagle betwixt them, currently looms above me, showering me with a buzzy blue light. How acidly appropriate (to crib the aa-alliteration). And now that I think about it, how ironic too: AA. If you ever ditch the sign for a newer one, I know a rehab clinic that would love it. That jumbo sign hanging in the "group room" would make for the flashiest AA meetings ever.

They've closed the gate terminal—my TSA angel, alas, has abandoned me, has escaped to his mattress at home—so it looks as if this will have to be it for me tonight. My final resting place, hahahahaha

----

TWO A.M., YES. Not quite so lonesome as three A.M., the bittersweet hour that inspired so many blues songs, but near enough. Even in this overlit airport, beneath your radiant blue A's, dear American Airlines, one can't fully escape the seeping darkness. It's like black oil, flowing in slowly beneath the automatic doors. When the doors slide open the blue glow recoils . . . oh for chrissakes dear American Airlines, are you still reading this? Well of course you're still reading this if you're reading *this*—this sentence, I mean. It's just confounding and some-how heartening, at this point, to imagine *why*. Who are you? You there, alone, dutifully turning these pages of mine, some-where . . . yes, you. I presume you're in Fort Worth—that's where this letter is addressed—and, the more I think about it, probably tucked into a cubicle inside a sleek, low building on the outer edges of the corporate compound. One of those anonymous office-park buildings in which the sole splash of color is provided by the lobby Coke machine. Reading this is your job; for the moment, then, *I* am your job. How odd. I have my own caseworker in Texas! Howdy padnah.

I suspect you're young, or youngish; sifting through the cor-porate slushpile is the stuff of an entry-level gig, of the ladder's lower rungs. I imagine you think of your life that way, too: as a ladder which you've just begun to climb. Allow me to take a wild stab, with apologies up front for any errant shots. You're a native Texan, or at most an Oklahoman, Fort Worth's radius of allure being somewhat limited. As a corporate citizen, I suspect you're a traditionalist, a casual God-fearer, perhaps the recent graduate of one of Texas's fine universities. Maybe the Uni-versity of Dallas (I did a reading there once), or perhaps Mid-western State—a no-nonsense school, a sensible campus, one of those hatcheries for the big corporate pools. Yet you like the concrete virtues of working for a large corporation. The transparency of your future, the way it can be quantified, is a comfort to you. To be frank I envy you: You aren't victimized by your daydreams. I don't mean this condescendingly, mind you. Your bootstraps are sturdy, you've got a plan. Your feet are planted firmly on the ground. You've got the world tight by its tail, etc.

And yet here you are—what time is it there, what day?—reading this. When you tore open the envelope and slid out this crazyass sheaf of paper your jaw must have dropped and you must have wheeled your office chair to the edge of your cubicle divider, holding these pages in one hand as if weighing them and saying to your neighbor in the adjacent cubicle, "We've got a record-breaker." Maybe you said a "nutcase" — it's okay. Maybe even a reference to Jack Nicholson in *The Shining*, with his hundreds of pages of the same droning sentence. That one's out of line but, awright, I get the impulse. There was probably much astonished laughter traded between the two of you, and maybe you even showed this letter to your manager who wagged his head with grim amusement. Yet still you're reading. You could've stopped a long time ago. Maybe your manager even ordered you to stop. "Hey, (your name here)," he might've said. "Enough with the nutcase already." It's not as if you require further argument to fulfill my refund request. In your mind you long ago awarded me that check, solely on the basis of my Bunyanesque efforts. (Or is it only a voucher for a free trip that you're permitted to grant? In that case, friend, I urge you not to bother.) Let's not forget there are other, more crisp letters for you to read, to sort through, to respond to. *Dear _____*, goes your daily mantra, *Thank you for your recent letter to American Airlines. Thank you for your recent letter to American Airlines.* So many letters, so many judgments, so many names instantly forgotten if indeed they ever penetrated your brain. Plus so much else to do in life, oh the hours can't contain it! Your mother is calling. Your oil needs changing. Your aunt's birthday is Saturday. The folks at work want to meet up at T.G.I. Friday's again — hey, why not, they're a great crew. Your college pals are emailing — forwarded jokes and inspirational messages, you can't keep up. Yet still you're with me — for reasons known only to you, you're listening.

What a weird & warm feeling that suddenly swells me with! Like finally putting a face to God — or at least God's secretary. I can't help thinking of that scene in Karol Szczepanski's novel *The Drummer of Gnojno* — alas, never translated into English — in which the hero is out on the street hurling mad, foamy-mouthed curses at the stained-glass window of the church (which is not so unlike, come to think of it, your giant blue logo above me) when the elderly pastor emerges and, after hobbling down the steps of the entrance with his cane, asks the hero to please direct his curses at him instead. The hero begins, haltingly, but when he looks into the priest's eyes he collapses weeping into his arms and says over and over again that he's sorry. It is so much easier, after all, to love or hate an idea. Perhaps, then, I should apologize for my prior hectoring & harangues—for my own mad, foamy-mouthed curses. When I called you a miserable fuck, understand that I meant it collectively, not personally. Obviously it wasn't you who threw the track-switch on my life or even on my current itinerary. No, young friend, I owe you better. You've heard me out this far so it's time for me to start coming clean. I'm afraid I've been dressing the corpse as always. There's much I haven't told you.

- - - -

NOT SO FAST. A fella needs to smoke, okay? My doctor says otherwise but he's paid to say that. During my last visit he had me blow into a plastic tube fitted with a Ping-Pong ball I was supposed to raise by exhaling into the tube. I suspect it was rigged. That Ping-Pong ball struck me as curiously heavy. Perhaps a golfball in clever disguise? "You have the lungs of a 150-year-old man," he said, har-de-har. (I was tempted, in response, to quote a line from Bukowski—"It's so easy to die long before the / fact of it"—but reconsidered. Quoting poetry is the quickest route to a blank stare, unless you're in the sack with a lady in which case it's a dangerous toss-up. For example, I once heavy-breathed these lines of Lorca's (per Merwin's excellent translation) to Stella: "Your belly is a battle of roots / your lips are a blurred dawn. / Under the tepid roses of the bed / the dead moan, waiting their turn." Her unexpected reaction was to shove me off of her and accuse me of conjuring her gang-rape by skeletons. And she was a poet! Or had been anyway. To assure her of the lines' proper romantic context I had to scurry off to locate the poem in its entirety. "To see you naked is to remember the earth," I read aloud to her, "the smooth earth, swept clean of horses." Because Stella was a horse-lover, these lines tanked as well.) Instead of quoting Buk to the doctor, I cheerily said thank you though he obviously hadn't meant the 150-year-old-man crack as a compliment. Sawbones scowled at me which I found unsavory since, really, I'd only matched him jest for jest. Apparently it's fair to make funny only about bodies you don't inhabit.

When I got home I bragged to Miss Willa and Aneta that the doctor had pronounced my lungs "antebellum" which went straight over Aneta's head but sparked a crispy Post-it note from my mother: NOT FUNNY. Of course we shouldn't discount the possibility that my impious reference to days in Dixie "not forgotten" was what caused her to bristle, rather than my sinking physical state. Her emotional allegiance to the Old South is infinite. If she takes any pleasure from living in New York, it is in having her prejudices about Yankees certified with every fair-weather outing. Once she saw two tattooed lesbians—hardcore dyke-types, from Aneta's description—passionately making out outside a Bleecker Street barroom at noon. It so disgusted and disturbed her—the in-public element of it, I mean, the lack of decorum; Miss Willa is not entirely a ninny—that she went on about it for days, weeks. So I've naturally kept the livelier details of Speck's wedding from her. WHAT KIND OF NAME IS SYLVANA? she Post-it-asked. "Polish," I replied, and she gasped and rolled her eyes before remembering our dear Aneta's national extraction. Poor Miss Willa. Hounded by Poles all her life.

Speaking of Poles: I wrote earlier that my father's death was oddly unemotional for me, a statement that might benefit from clarification. To be frank it seemed like such a relief for him.

I sometimes wonder—less now than I used to—how he ever reconciled the arc of his life, how he ever sketched out that self-narrative in his head. The there-to-here story you mull while lying awake in bed at three A.M. watching a spider traverse the ceiling. Or while immobilized at some godforsaken airport. Just imagine, though, working as an exterminator after surviving Dachau, making & disposing of corpses from nine to five. Flipping the switch on the gas, that sort of thing. What an unholy struggle it must have been to keep from connecting the dots—little wonder he sneaked his victims away to the docks. And after losing everything, let's not forget: his country, his family, his faith, more or less in that order. How high his hopes must have been—must have *needed* to have been—for America. Imagine that brass band welcoming him to shore: *I want to beeeee in dat numbaaah.* What did he think he would find there—here? What must his dreams have looked like? But then it's possible, isn't it, that he had none. Merely blank hope, an empty canister to be filled with the secondhand dreams of a new and scarless country. The dream we call American: a house, a wife, children, an immaculate green lawn, those legions of darker-skinned people whose worse-off situation exists to comfort us about our own. (One of my father's ironies was his adopted racial attitudes—he tossed the word *NEE-gar* around like doubloons from a parade float and was a party-line seg voter. History, even scalding personal history, doesn't always transmit the expected lessons. Memory and meaning, I've found, often book separate rooms in the brain.)

But let's not fool ourselves that the American Dream sufficed. No, you didn't see him at night, not watching the television but rather looking *through* it. I'd try to play catch with him and in his distraction the ball would bean him in the chest. Sometimes in the early morning—like a farmer he always woke at five A.M.—I would find him alone at the breakfast table engaged in what looked like deep prayer but wasn't.

Back when I was an altar boy, and weighing a future as a priest as ten-year-old Catholic boys in New Orleans often did, my mother disclosed to me that my church-shirking father, "of all people," had been studying for the priesthood when "the war started." What a shocker, since my father's favorite English word was *goddamnit*. When I quizzed him about this he waved me away, offering only this: "I had a date with God but He never showed up." ("Henry!" my mother seethed, pushing me from the room. "Don't you dare say things like that to him.") That line whirled back to me five years later, after his death — specifically, when my mother and I were sitting in the funeral director's office, them trying to decide what to inscribe on the tombstone. It seemed like a fitting epitaph but I kept this opinion to myself. That my first reaction upon seeing him in the coffin that day — dressed in a suit he'd never worn, a rosary curled around fingers so begrimed the makeup couldn't mask it — was a proud, tender smile, rather than tears, caused me hot grief & guilt for years thereafter. But I couldn't help myself — all I could think was that he'd gotten *out*. Go, Dad, go. At the wake one of my father's coworkers from the import shop, a beefy Cajun guy with forearms like Popeye the cartoon sailorman, put a hand on my shoulder and said, "Your dad's in a better place, kid." The standard rap. With a nod I replied that yes, I knew it, thank you. But I doubt we had the same place in mind. He was thinking entrance, I was thinking exit. It's the same door but the sign makes all the difference.

But back to the smoking: For the first time since my absurd arrival here, I found myself alone on the sidewalk. Just me and the pavement and my little orange-nubbed cigarette and a red trash barrel onto which a happy sign is pasted: "We're glad you're here," signed by Mayor Richard Daley and endorsed by the Walgreens corporation. I was standing by the trash barrel, half-drowning in old thoughts *à la* those above, when the automatic doors behind me hissed open, startling the hell out of me. I turned to see who it was—hoping for company, I suppose; hoping for something—but no one was there. A glitch. When the doors closed, I turned back to resume smoking until the doors slid open and closed anew. After that I watched for a while but, observed, the doors wouldn't open. Not until I turned my back to them again. Hearing that sizz of their motor, I spun around and lunged at the doors and shouted *A-ha!* But nothing; no one. Such an odd & lonesome sensation. For a moment I thought how wonderful it must be to live in that angel-patrolled world of the faithful, the world of Cajun mechanics with bulbous forearms, of the Munchkin with her patient, hope-fueled vigilance, of the hobbled old priest from *The Drummer of Gnojno* and the not-twit in the WORLDWIDE MINISTRIES, INC. t-shirt who knelt beside me several hours ago and laid his moist hand on my own spindly, Olive Oyl–ish forearm. To see the opening and closing of the doors as evidence of angels' invisible guard duty, of their soft comings and goings.

How much simpler to lay one's head against an angel's chest and whisper, "Now."

– – – –

NEVERMIND. Let's check in with our correspondent Walenty Mozelewski, who is standing by in Trieste. Walenty, can you hear me? Will you please give the airline an update on recent developments there?

> The Bear was obviously weary of Walenty's shrugs and averted eyes. "I am asking you as my friend," he said, "and as my fellow fighter." Noting Walenty's wince, he said, "But I am not asking you to fight! Only to march alongside us, for a show of strength—not any use of strength, I assure you. Only your voice! Surely you can lend me your voice for a day? Surely you feel a sense of responsibility to justice —to mankind? We did not earn these wounds, me and you, for mere sport."

Though, forgive me—some background is in order, isn't it? I forget that you're not reading along with me here. It's hard not to think of those towering blue A's above me as akin to the Eye of Providence, that divine, all-seeing eyeball that adorns, among other things, our precious dollar bill—tracking my every movement, my every grousing seat adjustment—or more darkly Tolkien's evil Eye of Sauron, but then, strike that, I'm trying to be nicer. Here we are at page 192 of Alojzy's novel, and this is what has recently unfolded: Walenty and Franca, no surprise, have become covert lovers. She steals away to his room at her mother's *pensione* in the predawn hours where they tenderly couple under the musical conduction of Trieste's birds which have become, for Walenty, his primary interest outside of Franca. He leaves his window open and scatters bits & ends of bread throughout his room to lure in the birds, much to the angry dismay of Franca's mother who, ignorant of his motives (and even more ignorant of her daughter's daybreak trysts with him), chides him for his slobbishness. Sometimes in the afternoons he lies on the bed and watches the birds flit through his room. His life is like a misted dream of warm skin, the sugar-dusted trills of birdsongs, the cool seaside air, his postcoital coffee, and his afternoon beers with the Bear—the unattainable attained. Or something like that. It's all a bit Hemingwayesque but that's hard to avoid when you've got a wounded ex-soldier drinking away the afternoons by the shore. For what it's worth, Hemingway would've had Walenty shoot & roast the birds.

True, Walenty's money is running out, and occasionally he's visited by thoughts of the old life—of his two sons, particularly. He's had no word from his family in years but feels confident about their fates since he left them in the care of a cousin, a powerful black-marketeer in Warsaw. Or is it less confidence than indifference? Franca's two brothers are classic ruffians—one of them tripped Walenty at breakfast one morning, and though both brothers laughed and neglected to help him up Walenty convinced himself it was an accident and laughed along with them. Yet he can't help but wonder if this sort of thugdom is what life holds for his sons, having been tucked away with a band of criminals while the war ravaged on. Franca warned him about her brothers—if they find out about us, she told him, they'll . . . but he pressed a finger to her lips.

And now there is the Bear, who has revealed himself to be a communist rabble-rouser and a Tito partisan. Tito, the Yugoslavian bully, wants to claim Trieste as his own; the Italians, of course, have their own title staked. Tito's followers are massing for a demonstration, to be held two nights hence, and the Bear wants Walenty's support. Walenty, on the other hand:

"You don't understand," he told the Bear. He'd promised to walk Franca home from work today, and already he was late; thus he spoke swiftly. "I don't ever want to hear words like justice or peace or unity or victory again—not ever. I've heard them enough. They've been exhausted within me."

"You don't want justice?" said the Bear, less shocked than confused.

"Of course, but I want it to be invisible," he said. "I don't want to be forced to hear it or think about it or say it or, worst of all, to act upon it. I just want it to be, and for it to leave me alone."

"My God," said the Bear. "What did you fight for?"

"For *this*, don't you understand?" With a wave of his hand he encompassed the sea, the sky, the beer glasses on the table, the route he would walk to meet Franca. "For the skin of a woman and coffee in the morning. For birds. I fought to stop fighting."

"For sex and birds? You're mad. You're describing an animal's life!"

"Yes!" Walenty said. "That's precisely what I want. The life of an animal—a small, unbothered one, something humble like a mouse or even a rat. I want to eat and drink and sleep beside a woman and not think about yesterday or tomorrow—in fact I don't want even to think. I am owed this. I want only to be alive."

The Bear was quiet for a moment, drumming his fingers on the table. Then he suddenly leaned in, and spoke gravely. "Do you know how I spent much of the last few years?"

Walenty raised his palms. "I don't want to talk about the—"

The Bear's voice became serrated with a low anger: "You listen to me."

(The Bear has never explained his wartime service, if indeed it was service—only vague references to combat in mountains.)

"I spent it eating *rats*. We caught them in traps we made with sticks and large stones, deadfall traps that crushed them, and sometimes because it was too dangerous to light a fire we ate them raw. Once we found a nest of newborn rats and we were so happy because even though there was much less meat, the meat was sweeter. We pinched off their heads with our fingers and ate them whole. So do not tell me you desire the life of a rat. I have pulled their bones from my teeth and wiped their blood from my lips and I have stopped myself from vomiting so that I would not lose their precious sustenance. You know nothing of rats."

Now it was Walenty's voice that simmered. "You do not need to explain starvation to me," he said.

"But apparently I do!"

"You're not understanding what I'm saying," he said.

"I understand that you are a man and are tired of being a man," the Bear said. "But look at you. You are still a man."

That Walenty relents is only partly due to the Bear's badgering. (Yikes, pardon the furred word choice: The badger couldn't bear the bear's badgering.) Back at the *pensione* Walenty has been tutoring himself in Italian with the aid of Franca's schoolbooks, most notably a translation of Tolstoy's little parable "Three Questions," about a king whose fretting over a trio of questions—When is the right time to do things? Who is the most important person? What is the right thing to do?—gets answered by a hermit and a fellow with a belly-wound. The hermit and the wounded fellow aren't important to us, but this is:

Remember, then,

wrote Tolstoy (via Alojzy),

there is only one time that is important: now. The present is the only time over which we have power. The most important person is the one beside you, for no man knows if he will ever have dealings with another. And the most important thing to do is to make the one beside you happy. For that purpose alone was man sent into this life.

Which is really just a slightly more profound rendition of Stephen Stills's "Love the One You're With," but it's enough to convince Walenty he should grant the Bear this favor: that he should march with the communists to the Piazza Unità, that he should at least hoist a fist in the air for his new friend.

When they assemble in the late afternoon Walenty is startled to see a homemade coffin at the head of the parade. "We are reburying one of our comrades," the Bear explains. The crowd is much smaller than the Bear had promised—fewer than a hundred—which makes Walenty feel uneasily exposed, more like a soloist than a back-row choir member, though he gleans some small comfort from his lack of the red scarf that all the other partisans are wearing. One end of a banner—*Zivio Tito!*—is forced into his hands, and though he tries to protest, he's quickly stifled by the movement of the crowd: They start down a hill, solemnly chanting at first but growing more raucous and unruly with every white-helmeted Allied MP they pass. If not for the banner in his hand, Walenty thinks, he would steal away; but the banner would collapse, and his absence would be noted. He tries to ignore the Triestines lining the streets to watch their passage—old men and women sizing them up in hostile silence, their arms folded stiffly against their chests. Children by their sides with hard bullets for eyes. For the first time since arriving in the city Walenty feels noticed, *tangible*, a player in the city's history rather than an unseen & unfelt observer, no longer an imperceptible fugitive from another life. His escape, it occurs to him, has been discovered; and a coffin is leading him home.

At the Piazza Unità, where blinding glints of sunlight zigzag off the Palazzo del Governo's gold mosaics, the parade is intercepted by an opposing crowd of Italians, also chanting and carrying banners: a counterdemonstration of demonstrably larger size & heart. There is much shouting and fist-waving which soon deranges, up at the head of the lines, into spitting and shoving. As soon as the first punch is thrown (at or by the Bear, as it happens), an American Jeep loaded with baton-wielding New Zealand soldiers speeds toward the crowds—in reverse, for whatever reason. As the partisans scramble to avoid its path, the coffin dropping to the ground with a splintery crack and a thud, Walenty notices the man hoisting the other end of his banner fetching a long-bladed knife from a scabbard hidden beneath his coat. Taking this as his signal to flee, Walenty tosses down his end of the banner and tries to cut through the rigid line of Italian spectators massed on the perimeter. But he is tripped, then held firmly to the ground. For a moment his face is mashed into the stones until he is flipped onto his back, revealing his attacker. It is Franca's eldest brother, grinning. "*Shiava*," he says (*Slav*), and aims a loose glob of spit at Walenty's mouth. The spit smells of *grappa*, and it coats Walenty's nostrils and upper lip. Legs flailing, he hears his own wooden foot hammering the stones, the sound identical to the crack of the dropped coffin meeting the earth.

- - - -

ON THAT FINAL NIGHT of my life with the Stellas, after I'd staggered back home from the Exchange and been struck mute in the rain beneath our bedroom window, I hiked to an all-night diner on St. Charles Avenue that I'm certain no longer exists. The city health department was always on the verge of shuttering it—the famous story was that a ceiling tile broke open one night and an extended family of rats came raining biblically down upon the tables—and surely some Javert of an inspector was finally able to padlock it. The other rumor was that the overtattooed line cooks regularly slipped LSD into the eggs, but this was more of a hypothesis to explain the squeamish, loopy sensations you felt after a late-night meal there than a bona fide allegation, though anything was possible. The jukebox was stuffed with a comprehensive selection of Ernie K-Doe tunes and the waitstaff was almost entirely composed of young Russian women who in retrospect might have been imported sex slaves. They had a carnal but melancholy air about them as if sex was available but no one was going to enjoy it. I ordered some coffee but my hands were trembling so badly that I subsequently ordered some vodka with which to spike my joe. Per my usual tack when drinking, I ordered a plate of food but barely touched it. Throughout my life waiters were always asking me if something was wrong.

At the next booth, I remember, was a skinny kid in a black t-shirt sitting with a girl who was too obviously infatuated with him. I eavesdropped. The kid was a drummer and was trying to impress upon the girl the importance and sublimity of New Orleans rhythm. She was nodding, and saying *Mkay, mkay,* but the kid was on a roll, his Adam's apple bouncing like a backwoods preacher's, and at one point, painfully bored with the topic but not with him, she said to him, with a fluttering of eyelashes, "You're crazy, do you know that?"

I turned around to face them. "No, he's not crazy," I said to the girl. "He just can't love two things at once."

I was just trying to help. Or something. In New York I would've been told to mind my own fuggin bidness or worse the kid might've awarded me a cool shiner. But this was genteel New Orleans where even the strung-out drummer-boys were gracious. "Thank you," he said, with just enough sarcasm to gild the lily. After turning back to my uneaten eggs, which looked up at me with poignant yellow eyes, I heard the girl call me a "creep" and convince the kid who was "crazy" to relocate to another booth. I waved my fingers at her and said, "Toodleloo."

The creep stayed there until dawn but never stopped shaking. The morning might have felt cleansing had I ever ceased drinking, but I hadn't, and when the sunlight hit me on the sidewalk it felt like falling glass shards. I ended up at Felix's apartment. He was annoyed to be awakened but was otherwise hospitable, though not enough to put his teeth back in. He was wearing the kind of oversized t-shirts that coeds sleep in and I couldn't help wondering where a shopper might locate such an oversized-oversized t-shirt and what sort of mythically large *sasquatch* the Filipino textile-factory worker who sewed the shirt must have imagined she was dressing. It was a white t-shirt that was only a half-shade lighter than Felix's pasty skin; he resembled a snowman in mid-melt. Felix didn't ask any questions and immediately fixed me an Orange Blossom—what these days in New York is called a "gin-and-juice"—because he didn't stock vodka. His apartment was legendarily revolting (a former barkeep at the Exchange had anonymously telephoned the aforementioned health department to report it), with a rusted and trash-filled oil drum in the center of the kitchen over which three or four ugly tomcats fought for access, and porn strewn everywhere. There was nowhere you could sit without a glossy vagina or breast staring you vacantly in the face. These did not strike me as happy vaginas but then I was never any expert.

Always on the cutting edge of technology, Felix the Fat was eager to exhibit his new prize, a "videocassette recorder," and to demonstrate the pinnacle of its utility he popped in a video he'd just scored via mail-order from California. It was a compilation of scenes of men ejaculating on women's faces. "One hundred percent cumshots," said Felix, pulling a chair close to the television set in order, in those pre–remote control days, to control the action. Proudly noting the Fast Forward feature, he said, "Watch this one. In her hair! Oh, man. Genius." I noticed his teeth resting on the coffee table; they were aimed at the television, as if watching alongside us, and I feared they might come chattering to life to provide the play-by-play to Felix's color commentary. Some of the cumshots made Felix laugh and others struck him as tragic ("What a dribble. Lookit that. She's disappointed"). Others angered him and others filled him with awe and admiration. "You know," I finally said to him, in an inappropriately reflective tone, "it's never even *occurred* to me to do that to a woman." Felix guffawed and said, "That's why you got a baby and I don't," which struck me as the loosest possible interpretation of that difference between us.

Strangely, I found some solace in the video. Compared with the men on the tape, I was almost Lancelot. Even after Felix left in the afternoon, to open the Exchange, I watched the video —over and over again, actually. Not in the rub-a-dub way Felix watched it, the way it was intended to be watched—a *Captain Kangaroo* rerun would have been more arousing to me. Rather, it said to me: Yes, I was a lout, a ne'er-do-well lush, a narcissistic chaser of vainglory (What did I hope for, mailing my poems out to the world? Just who did I envision reading them? A crusty committee of award judges debating whether to hang a medal around my neck? No, I imagined a woman in full swoon, a brunette for whatever reason, clutching my poems to her chest and overcome with the sweltry desire to rescue me from myself), a man forever on the hunt for the easy way out, with an eye perennially cocked toward the exit. But I wasn't a beast, I told myself, I wasn't evil. Look at those bastards on that tape, I thought, just *look* at them. There wasn't hope for them but there was for me.

Later that afternoon I went back to our house. I'd showered and shaved though was unfortunately still dressed in the same clothes as the night prior, and I was more or less sober or perhaps to be accurate not drunk. I had a single slug of gin before I left, to steady my nerve. Or maybe it was two slugs, to reflect that my body was threaded with more than one nerve. The key was still missing so demurely I knocked on our door. I'd considered flowers but that struck me as such a wormy Andy Capp maneuver. Nevertheless I had everything in mind to say—the outlines of a Marshall Plan for my own reconstruction. I'd go light on the drinking, stick only to beer. I'd quit the Exchange, and get a better, *real* job—maybe at a bookstore, that sounded nice. I'd write only on the weekends, like a hobbyist. Stella had once suggested I "see somebody," as in a psychiatrist—what in those days we called a "shrink." Sure, why not. I'd need to reserve a few demons for my poems, I thought, but certainly I had enough that I wouldn't miss those a shrink might slice away. I'd even take up jogging if that's what it required: me with a sweatband on my head, huff-puffing down Magazine Street. Anything, I could do it.

No answer. "Stella?" I said. "Stella?"

From the bottom of the stairs I heard my name called. It was Robbie, our downstairs neighbor. He was a chef at a French Quarter restaurant, a turtle-soup joint favored by midwestern tourists. Wide-eyed folks wearing Mardi Gras beads in August, that crowd. Robbie was married to a painter named Sally, a languid, too-gentle woman who was difficult to converse with because negativity seemed to mentally bruise her. If you complained about, say, the rain, she'd note how it was all part of the wonderful ecological cycle. Nevermind that you'd left the windows down on the Caprice—blessed Gaia was having a bath. She actually enjoyed reading Thoreau—yeah, exactly—though I'm certain she never caught his jokes. Stella adored the two of them, however, and pointed to them as a model couple, as a condition to aspire to. "You should talk to Robbie sometime," she'd once suggested. "He's such a great husband, you could learn something." I noted to her that when I passed their doorway I almost always heard Kenny Rogers on the hi-fi. Case closed, so far as I was concerned.

"I've got the key for you," Robbie said.

"Oh," I said, jaunty-like, and padded down the stairs.

He disappeared into his apartment, leaving the door cracked enough for me to catch a couple of verses of an Anne Murray song. This was not a moment to be rolling my eyes but I rolled them anyway. When he handed me the key he said, "I'm really sorry about everything."

About what everything?

"Stella going out to California," he said. "She was pretty, um, distraught and, you know, I'll bet this is really hard for you. I mean, of course it is. Women, jeez-us"—slight cognitive dissonance, him saying "Women, jeez-us" with Anne Murray's voice backing him. "But look," he said, "these things happen. I'm sure you'll work it out."

I climbed the stairs in a hot muddled daze. At first glance the apartment looked the same. Robbie was off his fucking rocker! Or a sick joker. There were my books, here was our TV on its cinderblock throne, there were the framed photos scattered throughout the living room. Almost all of them showing Stella and Speck—as the photographer, I was always excluded from the recorded memories. For a moment I was relieved; I half-expected to encounter the symbolic whoomph of an empty apartment, stripped of even its meager furniture. But then I looked closer. Stella had emptied the bedroom closet of most of her clothes, save the despised maternity wear. Speck's drawers were vacant except for the onesies she'd outgrown. Her storybooks were still there, and her toys littered the floor (there was that voodoo doll, lying facedown like a shooting victim), but her very precious, must-have Baby Bear was absent from the crib. That absence was like the period at the end of an awful sentence congealing slowly into view: *They're gone*. Stella must have packed them up that night, after we'd fought, while I was at the Exchange slumped against B. B. Mike with a tiara on my head, and caught a redeye out to L.A., to camp with her parents. Maybe it was even an American Airlines flight she booked—a chancy stab at grim coincidence. For a while I wandered the apartment, conducting a stupefied inventory of what she'd taken and what she'd left, as if to ascertain the degree of her seriousness, the quantifiable finality of it all. Could she truly desert her copy of Sylvia Plath's *Ariel?* She adored Plath. Her scribbled little annotations flowered the book's every other page. Was life with me so terrible that she would abandon all her shoes? I put one to my nose, as if to capture a last fading trace of her, but it smelled only of ripe new leather. Plus I couldn't help wondering what I was doing: Feet repulsed me, even hers. Then in the nursery I noticed a little poop stain on Speck's changing-table cover, a narrow little butterscotch skid mark, and for whatever reason the sight of that snapped me, twig-like, in two. Clutching the edges of the changing pad, I shook with sobs—weeping over my daughter's crusted shit.

"Bennie?" It was Robbie.

"Yeah," I called back to him. I wiped away my tears with my shirtsleeve which smelled alarmingly of vomit. I searched for stains but saw nothing and all I could figure was that I'd drunk so hard the night before that even my pores had puked. For God's sake, was all this really happening? "Coming," I called.

He was standing in the open doorway with Sally beside him. He looked concerned; her expression, on the other hand, was decidedly prosecutorial. Owing to Sally's earth-mother garb —a blocky dress of batiked and embroidered cotton; a mutant variety of footwear falling somewhere between house slippers and garden clogs; and a rainbow-striped hairband—I was reminded of that old tagline from the Chiffon margarine commercials: "It's not nice to fool Mother Nature." Mother Nature looked pissed. I don't think she'd ever forgiven me for passing out in the bushes once and crushing some of her pansies. The broil of her current visage made me wonder if she'd helped Stella pack. "We just wanted to make sure—we just wanted to see if you were okay," Robbie said.

"Sure," I said.

"These things happen," he repeated. "Things will work out."

"Of course," I said.

Things didn't work out.

NOT A CHANCE. I placed a call to California forthwith. Stella's father, Frank, who was some sort of midlevel state judge and taught political science on the side, fielded the call. "Ben," he told me, full of sighs, "my daughter has been through a great deal and can't speak to you right now. To be realistic, I think it's going to be a while. I understand that there's a child at stake so this is not a simple matter, but I can assure you that Little Stella is getting the best of care. You're going to have to accept the responsibility for this and give Stella the time she needs to sort out her life. I happen to *love* my daughter"—the compare/contrast implication made vivid by his emphasis—"and I don't intend to see her suffer one bit more."

What I wanted to say, in response, went like this: You *love* your daughter? Well, how about this, Frank—she *hates* you, she fucking *abhors* you. Here, you want proof? Look, right here, Plath's *Ariel*. (Christ, how could she have left that book? And me with it.) Right here, page 42, "Daddy." Plath's best poem, so far as I'm concerned. See how the page is marked up? With three shades of ink, *three*. And here, take a look at what's underlined: <u>*There's a stake in your fat black heart.*</u> (Did you say a child was "at stake," Frank? Tragic word choice.) <u>*Oh Daddy you old bastard you.*</u> Come on, Frank, let's talk about your oh-so-tender affair with your graduate assistant. Who caught you, Frank? That's right, Stella, and she was eleven, and the grad student was *blowing you*, Frank, sucking you off in the family sedan. Here come da judge, how cute. Stella was just looking for her bike in the garage, that dainty pink Schwinn with the pompoms on the handlebars, you remember it. She was supposed to be at a friend's house, of course. I know everything you said that day, Frank, everything you promised her and all the spidery ways you begged her not to squeal to Mommy after you'd zipped up your trousers and told the grad student—what, to "stay put," to "hold on," to give you "a minute"? Yeah, she told me the whole story, Frank, and you probably don't want to hear why & how but it was one night in bed early on when her reluctance to perform oral sex had reached the point of noteworthy awkwardness and we lit up a joint with our backs to the headboard and it all came streaming out, a sad tale but one so coldly, coldly related. I liked the detail of the grad assistant reapplying her lipstick in the rearview mirror while you were pleading with your own little Stella. Niiiice, Frank. A classy bitch. What was that line of Plath's? Something about where Daddy put his "root." Well we know where you put your fucking root, Frank, right into that polluted, lipsticked inlet, into that cheap mouth that <u>*bit my pretty red heart in two.*</u>

That's what I wanted to say. But I didn't. Instead I said, "I happen to love your daughter, too."

Frank said, "Well . . . ," and hung up.

As it happens, that was the day I switched from buying fifths of vodka to quarts, which is really just a matter of efficiency but let's not pretend it wasn't symbolic. My AA sponsor, Dirk (his actual given name, believe it or not), characterized this as the day that I *justified* my alcoholism. Dirk was a high-flying wine journalist before crash-landing into the program, and claimed to know something about justification—drinking was his job, & a man's got to do his job, etc. Lucky for him he switched from the wine business to the saint business: Nowadays he runs a Chelsea soup kitchen and wanders the city draping blankets on homeless folks.

Naturally my whole Marshall Plan disintegrated when Stella left. Two days later I was behind the bar at the Exchange, pouring my famous "two for one" shots: one for you, two for me. I tried calling Stella again a few days later, hoping the cooling-off period might be finished. This time I got her mother and you can just imagine how *that* went. I had to put down the phone midway through the conversation due to me bursting into flames. I wrote Stella a few long letters—not quite *this* long—which went unanswered. Then one night at about three A.M.—that dread hour again; Christ, the blood & despair that comes spilling forth when that cuckoo sings thrice—I dialed California and in an exceedingly ugly & weepy stupor told her father that I had *rights*, I could see my daughter, Stella had *kidnapped* Speck, *stolen* her, that I was going to huff and puff and blow the fucking house down. "Ben," he said calmly, "you are your own worst enemy. You should go to bed."

"I know all about you, Frank," I said. Menacing-like, grrr.

He didn't seem to catch my drift. Or else he was a cooler tomcat than I'd expected. (I suppose I figured he'd instantly break down, cupping the phone and whispering in falsetto, "What? *What?* Oh God what do you *know?*") "Rest assured," is what he shot back, "that the pleasure is reciprocal."

In my pickled mental state all I managed to say was "*Vice*

versa," which didn't make a lick of sense, not even as a pun. Frank sighed and hung up so I yelled at the dial tone until that escalating chime sounded and that nasally female phone-voice advised me that if I'd like to make a call please hang up etc. That call was enough to get a rise out of Stella, since about a week later I got a letter from her. Handwritten, dated, distressingly formal. The Cliffs Notes go like this: It was over. There was no use trying to fix it and the only thing I was feeling right now was guilt, which suggested that I wasn't completely inhuman but guilt was still, in the end, a selfish sentiment and thus more of the damn same. I could see Speck only after I'd completed care at an alcohol treatment facility and made other assorted penances, and Frank—"my father," she called him, not "Daddy"—had a team of lawyers prepared to enforce all that. Graciously, I suppose, she did admit that I wasn't solely to blame for everything, but said that, "quite simply," she needed to get on with her life and I needed to get on with mine. Signed it: Sadly, Stella.

SO THAT'S WHAT WE DID. Sort of. Stella got on with her life, anyway. She finished her Ph.D. at Pepperdine and scored a teaching post at UCLA which she kept for several years before she met & married Jon, a public-schools administrator with two sons from a prior marriage, and then she opened a boutique nursery in Pasadena which is apparently quite successful. (Snazzy website, anyway. A hundred different varieties of camellia in stock.) I know all this because for a few years in the '90s I was on their Christmas-letter list—an error, I felt sure. Due to those letters, I know that Jon—the last name is Kale, like the spinach; hence, I've always envisioned him as a cross between John Cale of Velvet Underground fame and the Jolly Green Giant—is fond of flyfishing and mountaineering though a knee injury in '96 or '97 put the kibosh on the latter. He's also an amateur wine collector, so their family vacations tended to follow the route blazed by my AA sponsor Dirk when he was sipping himself silly around the globe: Chile, France, Portugal, New Zealand. One Christmas letter mentioned—ostentatiously, I thought—that "the enclosed wine cork" was a happy memento of that year's travels, but my letter didn't come with a cork. I even fetched the envelope out of the trash to make sure. Where was my goddamn cork? So perhaps my presence on the list wasn't an error after all. I imagined the two of them debating whether or not to tuck the cork in with my letter. "No," I could hear Stella saying, "he'll probably eat it."

And me? By now you know the bones of that story. The hardest part was what to do with Speck's disposable diapers, the ones Stella had left. There must have been fifty of them, stacked neatly in a wicker bin under the changing table. Charity Hospital couldn't be bothered with such a puny donation. I was sure that orphanages still existed but because they were no longer called orphanages I didn't know how to look them up in the phonebook. The local battered women's shelter seemed suspicious of my offer, as if my fifty Pampers were a Trojan horse that would grant me entry to the shelter so that I could knock around some broads. It was a year before I mustered the cold strength to put them out with the trash.

Just as Stella demanded, I did enter an alcohol treatment facility: a shabby but sweetly bucolic place upstate where vast herds of deer grazed on the lawns and where I once saw a bear though no one believed me. By that time, however, Speck was already out of college. In the long interim I made a somewhat harrowing mess of myself and decided, without really deciding, to act like the monster I presumed down-deep I was. Or that Stella thought I was, same difference. Shortly before I left New Orleans, I was fooling around with an equally alky divorcée named Sandra ("*Sahn*-dra"). She claimed to have been a model once but that seemed dubious from a visual point of view. She also claimed, repeatedly, to have blown Mick Jagger during the Rolling Stones' "Tour of the Americas" in '75, but, you know, same doubts. We'd float from bar to bar fighting and losing our shoes, like in one of those love stories from Bukowski. One night, while she was doing to me what she claimed to have done for Mick, I withdrew at the last second to do precisely what I'd seen those chuckling neanderthals do in that video of Felix the Fat's. I had to hold Sandra by the hair for a moment. "YOU . . . FUCKING . . . PIG!" she screamed, wiping her cheek with a shirt of mine she'd plucked from the floor. I suppose I thought it was going to make me feel better, to seal my fate like that. Instead I felt worse. To boot, it wasn't much of a performance—Felix would've given me a thumbs-down. Even as a monster I was hopeless. I apologized to Sandra and knocked back a few vodkas while, to make herself feel better, she told me the Mick Jagger story again. Sounds like a charming fellow, that Mick. Does a little leprechaun laugh when you tickle his balls.

LOOKEE HERE, dear American Airlines. Morning is breaking. As an old saxophonist pal in New Orleans used to say, when dawn would find him with a beverage in hand: The sun done caught my ass again. His name was Charley and he died of a heroin overdose ten years ago. I threw a surprise birthday party for Stella once that featured Charley, hidden in the bathroom, launching into a rendition of "Happy Birthday" on his sax. A lovely moment that made me feel like a king though Stella didn't feel like quite the queen I'd hoped she would. She ended up crying by the end because she claimed the guests were mostly my friends, not hers. I could have pointed out that she didn't have many friends but I wasn't that kind of dummy. Stella was a harsh judge of character and few people passed muster. The handful of friends she had were always under caustic scrutiny, mostly for moral trespasses. Whereas I've always been an indiscriminate collector of people who tend to float in and out of my life without much passport control. Years of bartending inure you to human foibles or so I've always suspected. A regular at the Exchange, a sixtyish fellow who'd once been a successful financier before some mysterious disgrace toppled him, used to say, "I'll talk to anybody, on three conditions. You gotta make me laugh, or make me think, or make my dick hard." After hearing this spoken the fifth or sixth time I asked him what happened when he encountered that rare human specimen who could achieve all three. "I propose," he said. Well, we never could keep track of his wives. The last one was Filipino; the unkind rumor around the bar was that she was mail-order.

Most everyone around me is still asleep, but miserably so — curled up on skinny white cots or cardboard mattresses or on the hard blue carpet, contorted in chairs, propped up against the walls & windows with their dry mouths open, like corpses after a shooting rampage. Corny pink light is streaming through the windows, transforming the dust motes into floating glitter. Like little sea creatures suspended in the water or whatever the stale analogy might be. The window-washers have already arrived — what a rough early schedule they've got, though some of them must be grateful to avoid rush-hour traffic. The sanguine ones, anyway. This one near me seems blithe enough. He's a short Mexican dude with a flat Mayan face, shining up the windows via a mop-head attached to a six-foot pole. I've always heard that interior housepainters suffer sky-high rates of alcoholism, the theory being that staring at varying shades of off-white for daily eight-hour stretches drives them to drink. I wonder how it is with window-washers, always looking in or out — at glassed-off worlds immune from their touch. Eight-hour blinks of ivory-taupe-oyster-eggshell-alabaster-argent-pearl, the hermetic seal of glass, the guilt of abandoning one's child to write laughably mortal lines of poetry: I suppose we all have our excuses, our *justifications* as Dirk would say—our reasons for wanting to escape life for a while, sometimes longer. Some just better than others. Ah, the window-washer's cellphone just rang. Someone must have called to tell him a joke because he's laughing like mad, damn close to tears. I can't quite make it out; I used to have a fair grasp of Spanish but along the way I lost that too. He's doubled over with rabid joy, & hooting so loudly that a few of the sleepy refugees nearby are grimly yawning to life, casting annoyed glances down Mexico way. Rise and shine. Ees morning in America.

Early in this letter I mentioned that I'd placed my one call yesterday, & that it didn't go so well. Let's just say it didn't go as well as the window-washer's call. I'd just been bussed in from Peoria. No one would tell me a cottonpickin thing, as Miss Willa would say. From the payphone across from Gate K7 I dialed Speck's cellphone. "It's Bennie," I said. ("Bennie!" she sang back.) "I'm stuck in Chicago," I explained. "Total nightmare scenario—my flight didn't even make it here. We landed in Peoria and they made us walk to O'Hare. Well not really, but close. Anyway, everything is canceled. It's a complete effing mess." (Did you catch that? Me tidying up my language for my daughter.) "They won't say when I'll be en route but it's not looking promising for tonight—"

"*Shit*, Bennie," she said. Her voice was different: pricked, strained, impatient. I hoped it was just prenuptial jitters, or some knotty tangle of a wedding detail she was dealing with, or that maybe my ears were overattuned, my antennae too sensitive.

Nope. "We had a deal," she said.

"Which I'm doing everything short of hijacking a plane to keep my end of," I said. "And if you need me to do that, I will." How? I thought of Woody Allen, in *Take the Money and Run*, trying to escape from jail by carving a gun from a bar of soap. A decent tactic save for the rain that reduced the gun to bubbles.

"I'm sorry, Mom is being a total nightmare about *everything*" —"total nightmare scenario," meet "total nightmare." "One of Syl's law-school friends is stuck at O'Hare, too," she went on. "The two of you should get together to commiserate or something. Jesus, Bennie, I don't know . . . this is all getting a little weird and uncomfortable. Maybe we should just skip the whole walking-down-the-aisle thing and play everything by ear tomorrow, okay? Just say hello and start from there? Maybe not rev the engine so high at the get-go?" Another automotive metaphor, I noted: Perhaps a daub of the sludge that used to crust my greasemonkey father's hands had found its way onto the DNA. "Just get here as soon as you can, okay? Oh wow, I think Syl's brother just walked in. (Is that Wyatt? Ohmigod, just a sec.) Bennie I gotta go. Get those planes moving, 'kay? Chop chop."

Transcribed like that, it doesn't sound too bad, does it? Honest but genial, even a little hippy-dippy: That's my girl. No, you had to hear the clenched tone of her voice, the way her words groaned to a stop—I was just one more wedding headache (a wed-ache?), another abrasion in her life. But then what did I expect? A long time ago I'd recused myself from that life, confident that she was better off without me—or was I just, as I suspected of Walenty, *indifferent* to her existence? Over the years, in rare semisober moments, I wrote her letters that tried to explain my absence but inevitably I got soused and scrunched them into the trashcan. But, Christ, listen to me—how I hate it, that droning & hollow refrain: *I wuhzzz drunnnnnnk.* It's too easy to stuff the story of my life into a bottle like some rinkydink toy ship. One of those things you see at the souvenir shop and say, gee, how'd they fit that *in* there? It's a gimmick, an old trick, don't buy it. I think it was Seneca who said that alcohol doesn't create vice—it merely brings it into view. One of those dainty pearls of wisdom I found in the rehab-clinic library. I've got enough for an elegant necklace.

After she hung up I banged the receiver against the payphone three or four times—slowly, and with mounting force, my eyes shut so tightly that I wouldn't have sensed the flash of a nuclear blast rocking Chicagoland. *We had a deal.* No doubt I would've bashed the phone further, would've smashed it down to its wiry guts, had a retiree at the payphone beside me, wearing a t-shirt reading SNOWBIRD AND PROUD, not exclaimed, "Whoa, buddy, whoa there, what the hell?" At that point I wanted so desperately to kick something that I hopped around on one leg with the other leg cocked and loaded for bear. But the only things to kick were the wall and the Proud Snowbird and since both seemed innocent, down went my leg. That's when I felt the collective gawks of my fellow passengers at K7, bemused and slightly alarmed, zeroing in on me. "You got a problem there, buddy?" said the Snowbird Who Was Proud. An excellent question that I could have answered at length but chose not to.

Instead I fell into the closest O'Chair I could find, frightening off a woman and her toddler son in the seats across from me. Fine, go—that's right, I'm infectious. Or I'm the bogeyman. Not a terrorist though. Oh, for chrissakes all of you stop looking at me. Lou Dobbs of CNN is up on the TV screen accusing Mexican immigrants of spreading leprosy—you people want crazy, watch him. Hands trembling, I fetched a white legal pad from my satchel and began writing: *Dear American Airlines*, and so on & so forth etc.

— — — —

JESUS FUCKING CHRIST, you want to see trembling hands? Look at this, it's like my mother's shaky stroke-scrawl, I can't even make the damn words—dear American Airlines, you pigs, you *pigs*, you grabby fucking pigs! Just a few minutes ago—for fuck's sake, the *sun* is barely up—officers of the Chicago Police Department commenced to roaming the airport shouting for everyone to wake up and give back their cots because, as they thunderously explained, "the airline needs its gates." Screw your gates! To think of that poor old Munchkinette with the vegetative husband being rousted from her sleep by the fuzz! How dare you?

That's the exact question I asked one of the cops but it didn't go over well at all. He was a young crewcut guy, with a severely acned face suggesting that his muscle-lumpy phy- sique was derived from chemical supplements, with shallow blue eyes spread too far from one another on his face, skin like a raw bratwurst. "Hey, have some manners here," I said to him. "These people are just sleeping. They've had a rough night. You don't need to shout at them." Spoken without a touch of menace or hysteria, I can assure you. I know I haven't slept in the last thirty-some hours or so but I'm not entirely cracked.

"Back up, sir," the cop growled at me. I was a full yard from him. Any farther back, I would've needed to email him.

"How dare you treat these people this way?" I said. "This isn't their fault. It's the airline's fault. If the airline wants its gates, it can put us on planes." The cop muttered something into the miniature radio-mike on his shoulder and then said to me, booming, "Sir, I am *ordering* you to back up, and get out of my face." "I'm not in your face," I said. "And you don't need to shout at me either." Okay, to be accurate I probably should've pinned an exclamation point onto the end of that last sentence; by this time I was admittedly flustered. "Back off, *NOW!*" he roared, and in my peripheral vision I saw two or three other cops moving sharply our way.

I looked down at his gun. It was a chunky, square-handled

pistol of what type or caliber I can't say. The holster was made of smooth black leather, resembling more an oversized cell-phone case than the elongated, pantsleg-shaped cowboy holsters that I strapped onto my belt as a child, the kind embossed with horsey scenes that I would've sported while riding my own Cooch through New Orleans. It didn't appear to have the expected strap over the gun's handle; I looked for a telltale snap or somesuch, but the gun seemed wantonly unsecured, like a hand inside a loose mitten. So it wouldn't be hard, I thought. Just grab it. Distract the beefheaded cop by actually getting in his face and just—grab it. He'd go flailing backwards once the pistol was mine, whooping into his shoulder microphone, while the other cops would stream forward with their guns drawn, snapping commands; in a moment they'd have me surrounded in a semicircle. *Put it down NOW put it DOWN*. And then all I would have to do—how simple it would be, how ludicrously simple—is raise the gun in the air—not straight up, not aimed directly at the ceiling; at more like a forty-five-degree angle, high enough for the bullet to whiz over everyone's head but low enough to make everyone duck—and fire. Bang. Once, twice at the most. That's all it would take to bring a hail of bullets upon me. It was so easy to imagine: micro-mists of bloodspray popping across my shirtfront as my body filled with holes, that pretty pink morning light streaming like bright lasers through my perforated torso, me slowly swaying, swaying like a drunk maudlin dancer on an otherwise abandoned dancefloor, that same skewed light catching the bursts of smoke from all that gunfire, each little cloud curling out of the barrel and drifting into the next cloud as they spiraled upwards toward the ceiling. Nothing could be simpler. And all it would take is one quick movement, hardly a gymnastic one. I bit my lip and stared.

For too long, though. By the time I finished picturing it, I

had cops close on all sides of me. One of them was a short La-
tina, damn close to midget size, who put a gentle hand on my
biceps and said, "You need to sit down, sir."

"These people didn't do anything wrong," I said, startled to
hear my voice breaking.

"Just go sit down," she said. I did.

– – – –

WELL. LOOKS LIKE I'VE spilled the beans with that episode.
Or "come clean," as I believe I phrased it earlier. Maybe you
already deduced it, I don't know. Despite myself, I seem to be
scattering hints the way my father used to sow grass seed on our
little parched lawn. The truth is that I've been mulling it for a
long time—for the last couple of years, at least. Making my
exit, I mean: Bennie's great escape. Back in my twenties I used
to toy with the idea of suicide, but in retrospect never too seriously. Those were just hormonal doldrums, I suspect—swel-
ters of misguided Romanticism, overdoses of Hart Crane *et al.*
The dipshit insouciance of youth. I imagine we've all experienced those moments when we're in our cars and approaching a curve at fifty-five mph and the thought occurs: If I just
neglect to turn the wheel, fail to follow the curve—whoops,
the end. Yet there's a vast difference between wanting to die
and not caring if you do or don't. I've done both now—the latter for much of my life—and to be frank I prefer the former.
The desire for action—even final, irrevocable action—feels
so much better than no desire at all. The tingle of ambition
is still a tingle, even if the ambition is merely to quit. Funny: I
was surprised, once I'd made up my mind, how *comforting* the
idea seemed to me, the way it brushed the cobwebs from my
head. Once I'd decided it—this was about four or five months
ago, give or take—I found myself *whistling* as I moseyed down
the street, the picture of dopey contentment. I slept less, I
worked more efficiently. At times I played air-guitar along with

Minideth's floor-muffled solos. I even engaged in that clinical-textbook practice of giving away my belongings. To Aneta, mostly: rows and rows of Polish books, and a bunch of cool linden-wood boxes from the Tatra mountains that I'd brought back with me from Poland.

I'd never really figured out what to put inside the boxes, be-sides cigarettes and spare change, so this wasn't a dramatic liq-uidation. But Miss Willa noticed anyway. We are not generous people, my mother and I, and we're packratty to boot. Spurts of gift-giving raise an eyebrow. Of course you have to bear in mind my mother's own bitter flirtations with suicide; if any-one knew the routine, she did. I recall my father going haywire upon discovering that my mother had given her brand-new set of Tupperware to Mrs. Marge next door. She claimed to have developed a distaste for the color but my father, unconvinced, launched an inquisition. Ignorant of the subtext, I thought my father was being quite the miser. But he knew the terrain. Back in those days she would lie in the bathtub slicing at her wrists with a paring knife, but never quite deeply enough to crash through to the other side. I remember my father carry-ing her out to the car one summer night, wrapped in a blood-stained sheet. This predated the Tupperware incident by a few years—I must have been six or seven. It was dusk, I remember; she'd sent me to bed early for no valid reason I could discern. This upset me, because an early bedtime was usually punish-ment for some misdemeanor or other, and to my knowledge I hadn't done anything wrong. I'd even eaten the fried soft-shell crabs she'd served for dinner which was noteworthy since I was convinced they were actually battered spiders.

My bed abutted the wall with a window overlooking the front yard, and I was sitting at the open window watching some boys playing baseball in the street beneath the old green oaks. The neighborhood mothers kept chipping away at the game by calling their sons home, and when the third-base runner got beckoned—"Willie!" his mama yelled. "Red beans!"—the other boys catcalled him for a while ("Red beans," they chided after him, "rehhhhhhhd beans!," Willie waving them off with his baseball glove, shuddup) then turned their attention back to the game. "Okay," one said. "Ghostman on third." And I remember thinking how magical that seemed to me, a *ghostman* on base, and then, as more mothers called, more ghostmen entered the game, until finally the boy with the bat was called in and then it was only ghostmen beneath the firefly-specked oaks—ghostmen that no one could see but me, watching them round the asphalt bases from my skybox above, my face pressed lightly to the windowscreen.

I heard the frantic clump-clump of my father on the stairs but, charmed by the vapors of the baseball game, I didn't stir. And then I heard the front door slam and saw my father below me, carrying my mother the way new brides get carried across the threshold in old movies, and I heard my mother's weak sobs as he dumped her into the backseat of the car and then peeled out of the driveway. Ripped in two by fear and dread, I screamed after them—I *wailed* out the window, clawed at the screen. I don't know if I understood she might die, though by that time my grandfather had already passed so I was familiar with the mechanics of it—what I knew was that she'd suffered another "accident," and it took a long terrible time for her to recover from those accidents. Long chaotic stretches when my grandmother would move in and my father would drive me to the hospital every Saturday to visit my mother who would ask questions about the toy trucks or plastic army-men I'd brought with me but who would break into unexplained sobs when I'd try to answer. I remember removing my pillow from its case that night, after my shrieks had subsided, and putting the pillowcase over my head. It wasn't an attempt to suffocate myself, but rather an effort to shut out the world as completely as I could—to ensure that when I opened my eyes, I would see nothing, not even a ghostman. This was my analgesic: pure blackness.

My mother's too, I suppose. Back when I was hospitalized, she flew up from New Orleans and sat by my bedside letting all the stories spill out, her long and melancholy rap sheet. I'm not sure what her precise intention was—I had enough on my mind, thank you—but I think she blamed herself for my demise, at least partly, and figured it was time to fess up. She even told me—and this caught my attention—that she'd tried to take me out with her once. I was just shy of two years old the day she sat us down on the St. Charles streetcar tracks—"We were dressed to go shopping," she said, recalling even what shoes I was wearing (Buster Browns)—and rocked me gently in her arms while waiting for the streetcar to obliterate us. Dumbly, of course, because the streetcars have brakes, but then she wasn't thinking rationally. After just a few minutes a cop spotted her, which led to a year in an institution but no criminal charges. I have no memory of it, and it seemed to me then impossible to imagine: a toddler pointing down the tracks saying, "Train? Train?" and his mother—*my* mother—whispering, "Yes, darling, train," with mascara streaked across her wet cheeks. "Yes, dear, the train is coming." For a very brief moment, after she'd finished, I was incensed by this story—after all those years of warped bullshit, carting me off to Florida and Atlanta and New Mexico and then finally, when I was fourteen, to Saskatchewan (which really teed off my father, because he could never pronounce Saskatchewan; he gave up and called it Alaska), poisoning me against my poor damn father, poisoning me against everything, really, save some tweedledee vision of artistic/Romantic fulfillment cribbed from a flagrant misreading of *Madame Bovary*—now I learn she'd once tried *killing* me. But when I looked at her from my hospital bed, sitting on the edge of that aluminum folding chair, her rings clacking together as she wrung her hands inside out, I felt only a terrible, crushing pity. I extended my arm to her, which she used to wordlessly sponge her tears for at least half an hour. "It's a disease," she said then, "and I don't know why we have it. Why couldn't I have cancer instead?" I remember looking around the hospital room, as blue-gray and sterile as this airport, and saying quietly, "Yes, cancer would be nice." The pair of us, two whales unable to find a shore on which to beach ourselves.

So I should know better, right? Maybe. As I said about my father's weird strain of racism: History isn't always the best teacher. And as cockeyed as I'm sure this sounds, I can't help feeling that my mother's long sorrow stems from her *failures:* her inability to push through to the end, to reach the pure blackness of that farthest Faraway. Like that feeling I had when after three days in the coma I woke up with a tube down my throat: Oh, shit. *Now* what? Thanks but no thanks, as Stella would say. I closed my eyes but I was still there. I'm doing my best not to wax maudlin here, but really, what's the point? Please. You there, in Texas, with your future bright & shiny as a gleaming new nickel, you with the 401(k). Tell me what to do & why. Focus on my work? On unscrambling second-tier Polish lit for the two hundred or so readers halfheartedly clamoring for it? (Hunkering down on my job was what one counselor advised. I asked if he ever read poetry. "Well, not for enjoyment," was his answer. That helped.) So then, what—take up a hobby, get a puppy, instigate pinochle games with my half-collapsed mother? In *Darkness Visible* William Styron wrote that hearing Brahms's Alto Rhapsody (Op. 53) was what stayed his own shaking hand, fomented his own key change from minor to major. Naturally I went out and bought it. Halfway through I got bored and retired to the kitchen for a glass of skim milk, yum. Hearing the music bleeding from my open office door, Aneta ventured that it was "bool-tiful." I sent the CD home with her and Styron died anyway.

The thing is: My plans were all in place—vaguely, anyway;

I hadn't yet decided the means of my exit—until Speck's in-vitation arrived, providing an unexpected wrench. The more I thought about it, though, the more I liked the way it fit into my scheme—my "exit strategy," as pundits say about wars. At first I thought I would merely attend the ceremony. I figured this might somehow seal it for me, to see the evidence of my squandering—to confirm my own meaninglessness with it, owing to my footnote of a presence, A, and B, to afflict my-self with the sight of the path not taken. Like when a contes-tant on the old *Let's Make a Deal* show picked Door #1 behind which was a worthless zonk and then Monty Hall revealed the jawdropping prize behind Door #3 inspiring said contestant to want to gouge out her eyes with a hotel icepick. Less selfishly, however, I thought this might afford me the opportunity to tell Speck I was sorry, and to say farewell. And for what it was worth, to say the same to Stella. Part of me feared that this was cruel—how dare I reenter Speck's life in the last days of my own?—but another part of me rejoindered: At least you'll have made your peace with her. Better she remember a human than a sour mystery—a ghostman on third. But then I remembered that old promise I'd made to her, when she was really just a speck, that riff about walking her down the aisle one day, and I thought: Bingo. Wouldn't it be grand to fulfill *one* pledge in life, to reach at least one destination in this snarled journey? To go out on a high note, as it were. To do *something*—however small, and maybe, to everyone but me, however hollow—be-fore quitting the game. Envisioning it, I felt this sweet warm peace washing through me, an unfamiliar sense of composure. Nothing quite like happiness, mind you—more like the sat-isfaction you get when you tidy up your desk and clear a path for the day. In the weeks that followed I gave more and more of my belongings away, even the fancy stereo in my office that had failed, despite its crystalline transmission of Brahms's Alto Rhapsody, to toss me a life-ring. I left it in the downstairs hallway affixed with a sign reading FREE TO GOOD HOME. (Almost instantly I regretted that, however, because I find it damnably hard to work without music playing. Creature of habit, I suppose. I moved my clock radio into my office but that sounded like hell unless I stood there holding the wire antenna out the window.)

To be honest, I'm considering doing it out there. Not actually *in* California, mind you; on top of everything else, that strikes me as just plain rude. No, I've got Nevada in my head. There's no waiting period for buying handguns, & no license/permit restrictions either, plus there's all that gorgeous desert. Can you imagine? You follow a gravel road out to where it ends, miles and miles and miles from nowhere—beyond the beyond, as they say, the real Faraway. Leave the keys in the car and start walking. Just pick a direction and walk. The place to stop will be obvious. I've got the top of a cliff in my head, someplace with a vast and soulshaking view of the desert, all that beige nothingness splayed out before me. I'm thinking a drink might be nice, too—one last vodka-tonic to accompany the sunset. No wagging your finger. I'll pick up one of those medicine-dropper-sized airline bottles—maybe I can score one on the plane. But nothing bigger, no: You want a clear head at a moment like that. And then once the sun goes down, I'll lie back on the rocks and check out the stars for a while. I imagine they're something out there, like in New Mexico. I won't spook you with the rest. Just picture the stars—that's what I'm doing.

The "easy way out," people always sneer. What a crock. My mother had just gotten up when I was readying myself to leave for the airport yesterday morning. She was sitting in her wheelchair while Aneta combed her hair. Aneta sings to her, lightly, when she does this—sweetened, slow-mo renditions of classic rock songs, usually. She can make Foghat's "Slow Ride" sound like a nineteenth-century Polish lullaby. I asked Aneta to give us a minute, which puzzled them both.

"So I'm on my way to the wedding," I said, and Miss Willa nodded. Her eyes were on Aneta, straightening the photos on the wall to occupy herself as she waited outside in the hallway. I'd never sought privacy from Aneta; my mother sensed something was amiss. "The car should be here any minute," I said.

Miss Willa looks so old and fragile with her hair down like that—so raw with age, with all those coarse, bone-colored strands hemming her face. So damn helpless, is what I mean. But she'll be okay: We made a decent bundle from selling the ancestral home, pre-Katrina. I've done the math. I added her name to the lease. I even added her to my bank account so that she could cash any checks payable to me post-you-know-what (note: this means my refund check from you). And she'll understand—peas in a pod, all that. "Okay, then," I said, and then, somewhat to my surprise, my eyes began welling with tears. Well, shit. I didn't want her to see this, so I took her head in my hands, aiming her gaze downward, and bent down to kiss her forehead. I said, "I love you, no matter what," then I planted my lips on her forehead for much longer than I'd intended because I couldn't seem to detach myself. We're not prone to soft moments like this and I can't deny that a small part of me wanted to bite her—not to wound her, necessarily, but to suck out that poisoned brain the way frontiersmen used to suck the venom out of a rattlesnake bite, pa-tooey. Or maybe to wound her, let's be honest. For a moment, the scent of her freshly washed hair reminded me of the wisteria bush that sprawled beside our garage in New Orleans and sugared the springtime air, but this was just an olfactory illusion, a doleful trick of the mind. It was only old-lady shampoo from the Duane Reade sale rack. It had nothing to do with my life.

When finally I stood back up I could tell my bluff had failed

—I saw confusion and fear pooling in her eyes. She fetched her Post-it pad and pen from the side pocket of the wheelchair and wrote me a short frantic note which I folded and slipped into the inside pocket of my coat. "The car service is here," I said, though it wasn't, and with her bony hand in mine I kissed her forehead again, this time crisply, with the softness and brevity of an alighting housefly, before walking down to the street where I sat atop my suitcase with my head in my hands. My driver was from Bangladesh, said he had relatives in California. Midway up the FDR Drive I unfolded my mother's note. No, it said. That was all. I stared at it for a long while, watching it darken as the car dipped into tunnels below buildings then watching the sunlight flame it in my hand when we emerged from the gloom. No. At first the driver didn't mind me smoking but finally on the Triborough Bridge he said enough was enough. "Please, sir," he begged. "Please no more."

- - - -

THIS JUST IN:

"The earliest we can get you out is on the 11:15," said the ticket agent, name of Keisha.

"Arriving when?"

"Let's see"—click, tap, click of her keyboard—"1:35."

"No, no, that's too late," I said. "I have a wedding at two. There's no way for me to make it in time."

"Sir, I'm sorry but that's the best we can do."

"No, no, it's not. Look, I've been here since yesterday morning. I didn't even *fly* here—I was bussed from Peoria on your top-secret bus line. I haven't slept since Thursday. My sciatic nerve is so frayed from sitting in these chairs that I'm going to need my entire midsection replaced. I ate a hippopotamus turd for dinner. I was almost tear-gassed by the Chicago Police Department. All because my daughter is getting married this afternoon and I have to be there—I am *going* to be there. Quite frankly it's a matter of life and death."

"The first flight is at 9:50 and it's"—click, tap, click—"already overbooked. I'm happy to put you on standby for that one but your chances are pretty much nil. I'm just being honest. As you know we had a weather situation yesterday and we're doing our best to catch back up. Everyone here is in the same boat."

"A boat!" I said. "Like a rowboat—that'd be faster. Can you put me on a rowboat? I'll row."

"I apologize again, sir. I've got you on the standby list for the 9:50 and here's your boarding pass for the 11:15. Gate H4, boarding will begin at 10:45."

"I don't think you understand—"

"Sir, there's a very long line behind you and if I could get you out any earlier, I promise you I would. Gate H4, and thank you for flying American."

Slinking back to my seat I spied an American Airlines "Premium Services" cart heading toward me. Figuring what the hell, I flagged it down. If anyone deserved Premium Services, I thought, I did. I might note, however, that this sense of entitlement is atypical for me. Several years back I was hosting a visiting Polish poet of limited international repute who had a taste for American strip clubs. For "pole-dancing," said this Pole. We were ensconced in an "upscale" Midtown joint where bluejeans were prohibited—I happened to be wearing such, but, undaunted, my charge had dragged me four blocks east until he found a little cockpit of a store where he bought me a flamboyant pair of polyester slacks of the type worn by marchers in the Puerto Rican Day parade—and where you were expected to order Dom Perignon by the bottle while you ogled the strippers. It wasn't long before said poet was cuddling a girl named Cookie who asked if we wanted to visit the "VIP room." Now, I understand that access to the VIP room is available to any schlub with a hundred-dollar bill, but I still couldn't follow them there. I'm just not V.I. so why pretend? I waved them on. After a while my poet returned looking glum. Cookie had munched a Slim Jim while straddling his lap—struggling with his English, which he was adamant about practicing when stateside, he called it a "meat wand" which I thought wonderfully poetic & precise—and to boot he had lost a contact lens between her bosoms. As a man of the people, I felt vindicated. I wasn't Very Important but I still had my eyesight.

Anyway. Premium Services. A plump woman roughly my age was behind the wheel. She looked kind enough, I thought, with the sweet face of a cookie-baker. Not Cookie. A cookie-baker. V.I. Difference.

"Mind giving me a lift?" I asked.

"That depends, handsome," she said. "Where ya goin?"

"Los Angeles," I said. Noting her expression, I offered to share the driving.

"Sorry, hon," she said, with what appeared to be sincere reflection & regret. I got the feeling that had I said Cleveland she might've gone for it. She beeped the horn to get through the crowd, but it wasn't a horn sound—rather that digitized birdsong again. Her motorized sparrow flitted down the concourse and out of sight. My friend Walenty, I thought, would get a kick out of that. His dream car. The thought of him tooling up and down Trieste's hills in that little buggy, one arm on the wheel and the other around Franca, carving his way through the crowds by tweeting that avian horn—now there was rare cause for a smile.

- - - -

SHORT-LIVED, I'M AFRAID. Franca's brother is dead. Walenty's banner-carrying partner, the fellow with the long-bladed knife, saw Walenty being pinned down and spat upon and made a banshee charge. He grabbed the brother's hair and, after hoisting him upward, plunged the knife between his shoulder blades. Walenty's gaze darted between the two men atop him: Franca's brother, woozy and painstruck, flexing his arms sideways the way one mimics a chicken, as if to squeeze out the blade, then a ribbon of blood unfurling from his mouth as he toppled forward; and behind him his killer, Walenty's defender, for a moment looking as stolid and content as a butcher carving a ham, not even breathing very hard, until he was yanked upward into the raving crowd. To Walenty it appeared that he ascended, in the manner of saints, an impression borne out by the man's expression: His pupils went suddenly round, as if the abrupt loss of gravity was beyond comprehending, and then he was gone, chewed & swallowed by the crowd. Trapped on the ground beneath Franca's brother, Walenty viewed the subsequent riot as a torrent of boots and legs—kicking him, squashing him, leaping over him. For so long he had dreamt that bittersweet dream of his lost leg returning to him, and here now was its nightmarish obverse: a rain of useless legs.

If it hadn't been for Franca's brother's corpse, shielding him, he would have been smothered in the stampede. The New Zealand troops squelched the riot with a bit of tear gas and a great deal of whacking people on the heads with batons; then the medics moved in. Owing to his bloodsoaked torso, the medics presumed Walenty a riot casualty and delivered him to an Allied field hospital by a river. That's where we find him now. He's caught the attention of the man overseeing the local police force, a Kiwi colonel puzzled by this one-legged Pole discovered hiding beneath a corpse.

"Your name again?"

"Walenty Mozelewski. *Starszy kapral, Drugi Korpus Wojska Polskiego.*"

"In Italian please. Or English? Eh? Little bit?"

"I was a corporal. In the Polish II Corps. You remember Monte Cassino?"

"I was there."

"Me too." Walenty patted his leg. "Some of me still is."

"And now you are here."

"It was an accident."

"Losing your leg, you mean?"

"No, coming here. To Trieste."

"Please," the colonel said. "Explain."

So Walenty does. When he comes to the detail of Franca, the colonel throws his hands in the air and says, "Of course! A girl. It's always a girl. Dig down deep enough and I'll bet you'll find a girl was the cause of this whole goddamn war. Some German bird who wouldn't spread her legs for little Adolf, right? Brassed him off good. Go on." When Walenty finishes, the colonel offers him a cigarette and then lights one for himself.

"A case of *hamartia*, then," the colonel finally said. "Do you know it? It's a word from the Greek playwrights. An innocent act that results in criminal consequences, that's what it means. Like Oedipus bedding his mother and all that. Really a sad story, yours. You boarded the wrong train and now a young man is dead because of it. And now I have to deal with the mess of this young man being dead. Hot blood around here. The people, I mean. They're hotblooded. The damn Jugs are just the half of it. In the meantime, of course, you've got to go home."

"I don't have a home," said Walenty. "The Germans slaughtered it and then they divvied up the meat at Yalta. Now Russia is gnawing the bones."

"How poetic. Well then, you don't have to go home," the colonel said. "You just have to go someplace else. Up the boohai for all I care. But I fear I do have to insist. Considering the trouble and all."

"This is someplace else."

"Not anymore," said the colonel.

This is someplace else. Not anymore. Jesus. After smacking head-on into those lines of the novel, I closed the book and tucked it back into my satchel and went outside for a smoke. Probably for the last time, however, because the line through security to get back into the terminal area is coiled from here to Sheboygan. It looks so daunting to me, in fact, that I've reoccupied my former seat here beneath your towering blue A's, outside the secured terminal by the ticket counters—my old graveyard-shift perch. I need just a minute before inserting myself back into that snaked misery. I'm not quite prepared, yet again, to place my floppy shoes onto that stuttering conveyor belt; my shoes have been X-rayed so many times in the last twenty-four hours that I feel sure they've developed malignancies. By the time I reach L.A. they'll be three-eyed and glowing. And the indignity of sockfeet! Don't get me started.

It must be nine or so. I suppose I could ask to be sure. "Nine-oh-seven," the attractive young lady next to me just answered me after conferring with her cellphone. Though the sheerness of her attire might lead one to question her quote-unquote ladyhood. She's wearing a loose black tanktop of the kind worn by professional basketball players and it hasn't escaped my attention that she's braless under there. Earlier when she bent down to retrieve an *Us Weekly* from her carry-on I glimpsed her entire left boob in profile, a soft, inverted cone the same color as fresh buttermilk, with a delicious pink tic-tac of a nipple. The doodle on the left side of this page is the result of me pretending to write while cutting my eyes sideways. It's stunning the way a sight like that can completely derail whatever thoughts are chugging through your noggin. Even presumably focused thoughts about life, death, etc. To be or not to be. Should I stay or should I go. That age-old question ring-a-dinging through history. But then you spy a wink of creamy boob and everything falls apart. You're reminded that, familiarity with Slavic languages and theories of poetic closure aside, at your core you're just another mammal, hungry and horny, who'd be a fool to want to abandon all this. Part of you screams *More* while another part whimpers *Enough*.

The young lady's companion is a lanky, sour-faced delinquent in baggy, wounded-denim shorts and a black t-shirt that reads RAGE AGAINST something or other (I can only make out the top half). I hate to don my geezer goggles but why does this young generation talk endlessly of rage but never succumb to it? I haven't heard a bona fide howl in years. It's all spitballs from the back of the room. Not long ago I saw notice, in a full-page Food Emporium ad in the *Times*'s food section, of a sale on "Raspberry Rage Muffins" (four-pack for $3.99). So this is what it's come to, I thought. They're mixing rage into muffin batter. This particular young rager near me is preoccupied with his cellphone display (of course) despite his license to gawk at or even stealthily fondle the free-range breasts that have me in such a lather. I want to slap the backwards baseball cap off his head and shout, "Dammit, boy! Look at her! She won't be yours forever and there is no forever anyway so pay attention! Take her to the bathroom and fuck her until you're both squealing and laughing and so drenched with one another that everything else ceases to exist! Now! Now, dammit, now!" Like some carnal-minded Old Testament prophet in rags: Fuck now or forever hold your peace. Rage rage against the dying of the coot to your left. On the outside chance that he's her brother, however, I'll refrain.

I need to call Speck but it's too early there. Seven-something A.M., by my calculations. You have to assume she had a big night: hoisted champagne flutes, ebullient toasts, etc. Can you imagine if I'd been cajoled into giving a toast? Hardly a thing I could have said that a random busboy couldn't have said just as well. "Nice to meet you," would have been the gist of it. Then a glass held high and: "*Stella Gniech!*" No, it was probably for the best I wasn't there. I wasn't missed and let's face it I never was. Oh fuck it, maybe this whole trip was a mistake. Only now am I foreseeing the difficulties I've set for myself. What if she asks if & when we can get together again? Maybe she & Syl love New York. Everyone loves New York (except me). How the hell do I field that one? In my mind I've always envisaged her like her mother: as a well-bricked wall of resentment and earned apathy. *Thanks but no thanks.* Naturally I've rehearsed saying sorry & goodbye but always to inanimate objects. My desk lamp must be tired of hearing me apologize. Is it owing to Stella Sr.'s frozen rebuttals that I've assumed Speck will respond in a manner similar to that lamp? Notwithstanding the "we had a deal" exchange, she's offered me nothing but warmth. When I look at Speck's high-school photo, tucked incongruously into my picture album amidst flashbulb-bleached shots of me, boozed-up and drowsy-eyed, posing beside various Polish *littérateurs*, I can see Stella Sr. so vividly—even the wry angle of Speck's smile is hers. But I sure haven't discerned Stella in Speck's sunlit voice. A quandary, shit. Seems I've readied myself for rejection but not for forgiveness.

But enough about me. I fear my self-indulgent streak is more exposed than even my neighbor lady's teat. The fate I meant to address after smoking was Walenty's, not mine. What the hell does he do now? Franca is surely lost to him. He thought he could start over, could slide from one life to another as one flits from train to train in the subway—the poor fool thought he could escape. Imagine him now, roaming that New Zealand army encampment by the riverside. Wandering numbly through that too-familiar drab maze of canvas tents and marquees, guy ropes, latrines, ambulances, notice boards, gasoline heaters, stacks of empty ammo boxes. A black bicycle propped against an oil drum. A lone Kiwi lance corporal lazing in a chair tossing paper airplanes into the dirt. It must be getting dark by this time, with a fat pearl of a moon starting to dominate the sky. Walenty strays down to the riverbank—the sentry lets him pass; bugger it, the war's over—and sits awhile there, listening for any birds calling from the scraggly woods on the opposite bank; he hears only a few distant twitters that sound like a lost child, mewing in the pines. Alone, he watches the river blacken, a few moon-colored ripples fretting its surface. He tries likening his situation to the river's—"Perhaps the river," Alojzy writes, "knew things he didn't"—but he comes up empty. How many metaphors have we poets scooped from rivers? We steal them by the cupful, endlessly ballyhooing rivers' ebbs and flows, analogizing their fluid & imperturbable routes. Wordsworth on the Thames, etc. But in the end it's all dreck, or if not dreck then some form of bathetic aspiration: for our lives to course as smoothly, shifted but never stopped, draining into some glorious & storied sea. I'm reminded here of some lines from a young Grodków poet, name of Jacek Gutorow, about *the wind maneuvering in tree-tops / like a relatively poor metaphor, or maybe the metaphor / was accurate but life didn't live up to it?* Now there's a fucking question. Walenty flings a stick into the water and tracks its downstream float until it disappears into the gurgling dark. *This is someplace else,* he'd told the colonel. Please, he thinks now. Please, it has to be.

AT TEN-THIRTY, eight-thirty Pacific time, I dialed Speck's cellphone from a payphone nearabouts Gate H4. I got her voicemail and hung up. Dispatching the news in a voicemail message seemed crude but then again I had only fifteen minutes until boarding. Though more like thirty because, let's be accurate, boarding never starts on time. I wondered about those in-seat phones on the planes. I've never seen anyone actually use one, so perhaps they're merely decorative, like the orange

trees with inedible fruit you see planted all over Sunbelt subdi-
visions. Them oranges look swell but try just to eat one, blech.
Fearing I'd be the butt of some technological joke (the whole
planeful laughing at me for trying to place a call, much the way
a professorial chaperone in Tempe, Arizona, once cackled at
me for peeling an ornamental orange), I re-retrieved my calling card from my wallet and was about to dial Speck again, to
leave her my glum message, when the payphone rang. I leapt
back as from a hot wire. After a moment I concluded it might
be Speck—calling back the number that had appeared on her
cellphone—but couldn't be sure, so when I answered I said,
politely, "American Airlines."

"Bennie?" It was Speck.

"It's me," I said.

"Why'd you say 'American Airlines'?"

"Well, it's their phone," I said.

"Are you coming?"

"I am, but I'm going to be late," I said. "Too late for the
ceremony—I'm sorry." Until that moment, when I spoke it,
I believe I'd been harboring delusions that I might still make
it—that the plane would have a secret turbo function, that the
scheduled landing time was really just a worst-case scenario.
That somehow this was all still going to go as designed. That I
would walk my daughter down the aisle as I'd once imagined,
make my amends, and get outta Dodge. Saying it aloud, however, I felt my entire plan break into a thousand crumbs—*cake
crumbs*, I thought, courtesy of that line from Alojzy's novel
shooting across my mind, quick as a falling star.

"That *sucks*, Bennie," said Speck. "What time do you ar-
rive?"

"They say one thirty-five," I answered glumly.

"Then you'll make the reception, no prob," she said, as
chipper as I was forlorn. "That's the fun part anyway. You have
the address, right? The band we've got is amazing. The End of

the End of Love. They're clients of Syl's. They were on *Letterman* on Wednesday! Did you see it?"

"No, I missed that," I said.

"You'll *love* them," she said. "I can't wait to see you, Bennie. God, to *meet* you! Isn't that weird? There's a ton I need to know. Everything, right? Are you around on Sunday? The reception will be totally nuts so maybe you and I can have brunch on Sunday."

"Sure," I said. "Yeah."

"Okay, cool," she said. "See you soon. Oh wait, don't hang up, Mom wants to talk to you."

I didn't see that one coming at all.

"BENNIE," SHE SAID.

"Stella," I said back.

She asked where I was and I explained. Of course not everything: just the landing at Peoria and the jangly bus ride and the canceled flights as depicted on the empty, blinking schedule screens and the thwarted American citizenry sleeping on cardboard boxes with wadded-up clothing for pillows . . . and, in passing, and partly (I suspect) because my situation felt suddenly smaller, as if cast in a withering new light, the pernicious effect of the chairs on my back. The O'Hare Factor, I entitled it. "Seriously," I said. "I'm hurting here." She asked if I'd slept and I answered no though I worried this would make me sound off my rocker—which technically I am but why the hell broadcast it? Striking a sympathetic note, she said she hoped I had a good book along at least. I said I did. "A great one, as a matter of fact." I asked her how things were and she said "crazy"—but thoughtfully, as if things really were crazy. And then I said, "I hope I'm not adding to the craziness."

This made her laugh, or rather pretend to: *ta-HA*. I believe I've told you about that vinegary laugh. "Rest assured, you are," she said. Then she asked me to hold on while she ducked into another room. "That's what I wanted to talk to you about," she said. She paused for about the same amount of time it takes to load a pistol. "Okay, look. Here's my speech. Don't screw this up."

"Hold on—"

"I said it was a speech. Just listen. She's thrilled about you coming. In some bizarre way she's always idolized you, or at least some vision of you that I never had the heart to puncture. Or to be more honest the ability to puncture. You've always been like some kind of astronaut who was too busy circling the damn moon to come down to see her. She's pigheaded—you'll see. I'm sorry you're missing the ceremony or whatever they're calling it but I've got to confess I'm *extremely* relieved you're not going to be walking Stel down the aisle. Jon wasn't thrilled about that and neither was I. Mind me asking where that impulse came from?"

She didn't remember. The spark that set off the blast, & she didn't remember. Had I made it up? For a scant moment I panicked, fearful that some scene from, say, a nineteenth-century Polish novel, in which some numskulled fellow pledges to walk his infant daughter down the aisle one day, had lodged itself, shrapnel-like, in my soft and pickled brain. But no, I remembered. This was my life, I was there. This was where the road had forked. Had I perhaps overinflated the significance of the exchange? The lacuna in Stella's memory said yes but one must consider perspective. A piece of driftwood floating atop the blue ocean is hardly worth noting unless you happen to be clinging to it.

"Just something I got in my head," I said, close to a whisper.

Too close: "What?" she said. "Bennie, you're mumbling."

"You know how it is when I get something in my head," I said.

"Yeah, you always did put the pig in pigheaded," she said, following it with what sounded like a genuine laugh—a soft trill. Whether she was laughing about me or at her own wit was unclear. "It was a little *weird*, though, didn't you think? It's been a long time, Bennie. And not to be too literal about things but she certainly isn't yours to give away."

"Giving her away—wasn't the motive," I said.

"Well, moot point, right? Looks like the weather in Chicago saved us from that awkwardness."

"The weather here is *fine*," I said. "It's not the weather! What it is, the goddamn airline overscheduled itself into a corner and—"

"Whatever. Are you sure you're up to this, Bennie? Because she's not going to let you drop in and then disappear. That's not fair to her. You only get to run once."

"*You* ran."

"Oh, please," she said. "Don't even start. Please, *please*. And you followed? A handful of drunk phonecalls doesn't qualify you for martyrhood. But there's no use rehashing all of that. What happened, happened. And everyone's better off for it."

"That's one interpretation," I said.

"What's the other one? Come on, Bennie, we made our choices. Everyone does. You chose your barstool—the great saloon poet, right? While I raised our daughter. La la la. Life goes on."

"I ditched that barstool, you know. I tried to tell you that—"

"Jesus, you did, and I've owed you an apology ever since. That call couldn't have come at a worse time for me." She paused, as if deciding whether to explain any further. "I really *am* sorry," she went on. "I started a letter to you after that but for whatever reason it never got finished. When you called we were neck-deep in a terrible situation with Phil"—Phil was her stepson, Jon's younger son—"with alcohol plus drugs plus more than I want or can bear to remember and your call caught me smack-dab in the middle of it all. We'd just shipped him off to his *second* stint at a clinic up in Orange County, Jon was in the midst of selling his wine collection to get all the alcohol out of the house, and, no offense, Bennie, but you were about the *last* thing I needed at the moment. All I could think was: Great, maybe I'll get a call from Phil in thirty years saying sorry, Mom, had a rough go of it for a while, sorry for all that. I swear, what is it with you guys?"

"How is he?"

"Phil? He's fine, he's great actually. He's back in school with a respectable GPA. Has a sweetheart of a girlfriend he met in the program."

"That's good," I said. "That's good."

"How about you?"

"Oh, about the same."

"As Phil? Or . . . you don't mean . . . as before?"

"As Phil. Except for the parts about the GPA and girlfriend. But that's fine, you know. Miss Willa makes a decent prom date so long as the music isn't too loud and they play a rumba or two."

"That's funny," she said. "God, your mother . . . that's actually funny. I am sorry, Bennie. For a lot of things. I *did* start writing you that letter, once things had calmed down with Phil, but . . . I don't know, I'd put it all *away*, you know? It was all crazy back then, and it's so hard for me to recognize myself in those memories that I just—just filed it all away and locked it and tossed the damn key. You know, it's funny, one therapist said that was the right approach while another said it was dead wrong. So who knows?"

"They both cashed their checks, right?"

"Exactly, yes. Sheesh. We were just stupid kids. We made a giant mess of things but we survived, okay? And for all the operatic crap, Bennie, we made a beautiful girl. If she doesn't take your breath away then . . ."

"I'd give my life to take it all back, you know," I said suddenly, and hearing the faint, fleet echo of my words coursing through the wires, I asked myself—no, *demanded* of myself —if they were true. Because if they weren't true then there was no point to any of this, no point to me. But they were—all of them. A long silence swamped the line until Stella exhaled and:

"Yeah, fine, but you *can't*," she said. "God, Bennie, that's so like you. Offering up the impossible. The stupid ideal. It used to tear me in two. I never understood why life was never *enough* for you."

"I don't . . ."

A gate-change announcement drowned me out. Omaha, Gate H7. From down the terminal I heard spurts of applause breaking out, someone whooping.

"What? I can't hear you," Stella said.

"Nothing," I said.

"You know, a few years back—this was right after 9/11, and I guess you were on my mind, being in New York and all— anyway, I saw this science article in *Time* or *Newsweek* or one of those. This article about butterflies."

"Wait—"

"No, just listen. This biologist did an experiment and he found that if you put a male butterfly in a cage with a live female butterfly alongside a *photo* of female butterfly, the male almost always went to the photo first. And I remember reading that and thinking, my God, that's *Bennie*. Always drawn to that . . . what, that frozen image, rather than the real thing. Always stalking the dumb illusion."

Perhaps this was incisive—transcribing it now, I see her point—but what I gathered at that moment was that she considered me the kind of man who'd hump a paper butterfly.

"Sounds to me," I said, "like a biological explanation for the porn industry."

"Jesus, why did I think you'd take me seriously? You never change. Look, I have to go. Stel's calling me. Just come see your daughter, will you? Don't expect too much but don't do too little. She's enough."

I took a deep breath, filling my lungs with that stale airport oxygen. "I know she's enough," I said. "I mean I think I do." They were boarding my flight. The First Class passengers and Admirals' Club members had already vanished into the gangplank, none of them looking particularly classy and certainly not like admirals. Midshipmen at best. The gate agent announced that boarding would be done according to the "group number" printed on the boarding passes. Where was my boarding pass? Oh fuck me had I lost it? I tapped my shirtfront pocket. There it was, I had it, I was fine. Through the terminal windows I saw a plane rolling by outside like some great lumbering beast, some prehistoric meateater. "Bennie?" Stella said. I watched the passengers forking over their boarding passes to the gate agent. The permanence of the agent's smile seemed unnatural, painstaking. I refilled my lungs. Damn but I wanted a cigarette. A drink. Another chance. A soul scrubbed clean. A world made better not worse by my footprints upon it.

"I'm not sure the word *sorry* does anything justice," I said. "It's such a loose fucking word, isn't it?"

"Bennie, what are you saying?"

"I mean, how can one puny word like that encompass all the shit you did—I don't mean *you*, I mean us, everyone, me—but also all the, all the things you *didn't* do? It's the inactions that keep you up at night. The actions, they're done. They're done. The inactions, they never go away. They just hang there. They rot. How is *sorry* supposed to stretch across all that?"

"It's life, Bennie, not linguistics," she said.

"Is it? In Poland they say *przykro mi.*"

"Which means . . . ?"

"It doesn't really have an English equivalent, not culturally anyway . . . somewhere between 'I'm sorry' and 'I'm in pain.'"

"Say it again?"

"What?"

"The Polish thing. Say it again."

"*Przykro mi.*" Uttering the last syllable I heard my voice falter and I had to scrunch up my face to hold back a sudden torrent inside my head. I felt myself slacken and slump against the Plexiglas divider. "*Przykro mi,*" I said again. "*Przykro mi.* My God you don't know."

I heard Stella sigh. "You broke my damn heart, you know," she said.

"I broke my own, too," I said.

"Well that was stupid," she said, and when we laughed together my eyes brimmed with tears that were neither happy nor sad but merely wet.

I SHOULD NOTE that the preceding few pages were written at a cruising altitude of thirty-five thousand feet. In Seat 31D, to be precise. Dear American Airlines, I'm on my way. The seat assigned to me was 31F, the one beside the window, but I offered it to the pretty young Chinese girl who was occupying this aisle seat when I boarded. She doesn't speak English so I had to pantomime my offer of the window seat and for a moment the poor girl got all flustered, thinking she'd made an error. *Sah-lee, sah-lee,* she apologized. Since pointing to the window with a generous smile didn't yield me any communicative success, I sliced my hand above my eyes while turning my head to and fro in wan imitation, I suppose, of an Apache scout searching the horizon for invading honkies. This was my way of suggesting that she might enjoy the view. When she finally got my drift she thanked me profusely and after settling into her window seat cracked open a notebook that my wandering eye noticed was filled with English phrases written alongside their Chinese counterparts. "Where is Gate 5?" "Excuse me, can you help me with my baggage?" "Where are the taxis?" Etc.

It reminded me of the failed system I devised for my mother back when she first moved in, pre-Post-its. Into a spiral-bound notebook I entered every sentence I could imagine her needing to say, the idea being that when she wanted to express something she could page through the notebook until she hit the sentence she wanted, then point. I tried to be as comprehensive as I could—in addition to humdrum requests for food, water, medicine, and whatnot, which I arranged by category, I also listed generically critical opinions about television shows, a wide array of weather commentaries, and her own trademark expressions (e.g. "My hair looks like something the cat dragged in"). Under the "Miscellaneous" rubric I even included me-directed unpleasantries like "Watch your language" and "How is your work coming?" This phrasebook took me hours to compile—the plural isn't an exaggeration—so I was stunned and not a little infuriated when after a middling skim she hurled it, with obvious disgust, into the trash. Taking a ballpoint pen to one of my Post-it pads, she wrote on three consecutive sheets: I HAVE MUCH MORE LEFT TO SAY THAN THAT. I hadn't considered that it might be disturbing for her, to see the entirety of her remaining life—and what is life if not the words that we speak?—reduced to fifteen or so looseleaf notebook pages, sharp convenience notwithstanding. Thus began our Post-it note epoch. The era of LOVE IS LOVE and other uncollected tersenesses.

I shouldn't pretend not to notice the connection between reducing one's life to a handwritten phrasebook and reducing it to a complaint letter to a corporation that doesn't give a flying, delayed, or canceled fuck. Or stuffing one's autobiography into a bottle as I believe I said earlier. We all hope to be more than we are which is often the problem. What I neglected to include in my mother's phrasebook was something like hope—not the sentences she needed, but the sentences she *wanted* to need. *My recovery has been remarkable, hasn't it. I met a handsome gentleman today. Are those flowers for me? I would like two tickets to Paris, please. It has been so wonderful to paint again. We danced all night. I won't need this silly notebook any longer.* Take away Miss Willa's delusions and she has nothing. Banish the Faraway and she's lost. As the sole surviving representative of the life she's spent decades trying to escape, I could defensibly resent it all, but then what's the point? To varying degrees we're all victims of our pregnant imaginations, of incurable dreams of transcendence. Thorns hoping to become the rose. The religious among us, counting on seventy-two lustsoaked virgins and/or plump white raisins in the afterlife, or more locally reunions with childhood pets and predeceased spouses or the all-you-can-eat king-crab-leg buffet in heaven's cafeteria, are just the mildest examples. Think of Henryk Gniech, believing he could outrun the nightmares of Dachau by fleeing to New Orleans, or believing he was granting a merciful reprieve to those legions of varmints he abandoned on the docks. Imagine the terror of that possum, the one that resulted in my birth, as it navigated the hot maze of crates and forklifts and shirtless longshoremen on the docks, starving and thirsty, skittering up Poland Avenue in desperate search of food and water, or the comforts of a tree or a fellow possum, unstrung by the honking, swerving cars and the nasty schoolchildren hurling rocks at this rarely seen creature. See it cowering behind some greasy spoon's trash dumpster as night falls, motherless or childless, tremblingly alone. Which was the better fate? Maybe the answer is that there are no better fates. You can't escape what you are be it possum or poet. Maybe you get what you get. Or as the old saw goes: You buy your ticket, you take your chance. Which by the way you might consider for a motto.

On occasion—after the Stellas had left me and, stripped of Speck's physical presence, I was able to think of her more as an abstraction—I used to wonder how things might've turned out had Stella gone through with it. The abortion, I mean. I admit this sounds wicked but the devil's advocate is by nature devilish and anyway I'm not expressing regret—only probing the divide between what was and what wasn't, what is and what isn't. We would have driven home in silence from that clinic in Gentilly with a somber pitstop at a K&B drugstore to get some feminine pads to stanch any bleeding. We would've watched something on television that night, something silly and irrelevant like a Bob Hope special, me faking a cringe when Charo bounded onstage. Maybe I would've fixed myself a drink. ("Is that okay?" I would've asked, Stella waving her defeated permission with all the brio of an invalid shooing a mosquito.) And then Stella would have cried herself to sleep—I know her; everything unspooled in the dark—and I would have held her, stiffly, sadly, hurting in unlocatable places. And sooner or later the unspoken guilt would have wedged a divide between us, a gulf of sour air. We would have become, to one another, constant reminders of a loss, the salt to the other's wound. And then, maybe slowly but probably rapidly, we would have slipped apart. A fluttering eyelash in the Exchange, and the woman to whom it belonged, would have dislodged my stance like tectonic plates shifting beneath my feet; or a better man, named Jon, with tales of alpine glory, would have whisked her from me. What I mean is that maybe there never was a happy ending for us. Or rather, we had the happy ending—Speck—but it wasn't enough for us. Or rather for me. What I mean is that maybe it never could have been different.

Which is more powerful: that realization or a gun? It's all

so clear up here. At thirty-five thousand feet you can see the curve of infinity. It's all so possible.

As I write this the girl near me is scrutinizing her notebook. Every now and then she leans back into her seat and lifting her gaze to the ceiling she silently mouths one of the English phrases, to seed it in her memory. *Excuse me. Excuse me. Where is Gate 5?* Whenever she does this I catch a glimpse of the sky outside, and for whatever reason I find myself losing my breath, as if I am a child aloft for the very first time. Christ, my friend, do you understand how fucking *beautiful* it is up here? The clouds look like glaciers, cold whiteness extending as far as the eye can see and then farther and farther and farther into dreams. Imagine the first pilot to crack the cloud barrier—what a blind rush that must have been, to break down the door of heaven.

Dear American Airlines, I'm not leaving. I apologize for all your time but I've changed my mind. You can keep your money after all.

– – – –

BUT THEN I almost forgot: Walenty. No offense to Alojzy, but I've taken the liberty of rewriting his ending. I won't reveal Alojzy's actual conclusion except to note that it's violent and unjust—you can guess the reaction of Franca's surviving brother when Walenty reappears at the *pensione;* Franca's reaction is less predictable but no less brutal—which is how Alojzy has always viewed the world. Please don't feel cheated. *Nothing's lost,* to crib from James Merrill. *Or else: All is translation / And every bit of us lost in it.* With apologies to Alojzy, then:

> At the train station he ordered a cup of coffee. The girl who delivered it to him was hardfaced and curt and demanded he pay immediately. She tapped her thigh while he fished the change from his pockets. Soon afterward he saw her ar-

guing behind the counter with a young man in an apron who rolled his eyes at her with such frequency and exertion that he appeared to be suffering from vertigo. A small boy of three or four was merrily roaming the café and cocking his thumb and forefinger at customers as if to shoot them dead. Pow! he exclaimed to little or no response. When the boy's gun was aimed at Walenty he put his hand to his heart and tossed his head back which caused the boy to grin and jump and burst into a cheer. This caught the attention of the boy's mother who stood up from her breakfast and heaved the boy away by his collar. She dragged him beside her chair where she swatted him on the rump with enough force to make Walenty wince, spitting fierce words at the boy that Walenty was unable to understand save one: *father.* Stricken, the boy lay on the floor crying while the mother, eating small bites from a bread roll, ignored him.

Because the coffee tasted burned and oily and the boy's sad shrieking was soon intolerable, Walenty strayed outside to the platform. The train was late by half an hour and when it arrived the stationmaster charged out of his office toward the engine angrily brandishing a sheaf of papers. Among the passengers disembarking was a man in a heavy woolen suit and a fedora. He was carrying flowers and scanning the platform.

Boarding ahead of Walenty was a slender young woman in a lace dress, traveling solo. The hem of her dress snagged on a piece of metal as she was climbing into the car, causing her to slip backwards into Walenty. He caught her by the waist and holding her there, like dancers in a *pas de deux*, he reached down to unsnag the dress. It had torn just a little and behind him Walenty heard two women say *awww*, noting between them that the dress was real lace. When the woman in the dress turned to thank Walenty he could see that she'd been crying; her gray, longlashed eyes were rimmed with a pinkness like that of raw meat. She disappeared to the rear of the car but if he listened closely he could hear her choked-back sobs, random but persistent, at least until the train started moving and his ears were overwhelmed by the clatter.

The last thing Walenty saw, as the train left the station, was the boy. The man with the flowers had his arms around the boy's mother, the flowers, in his left hand, pressed hard against her back. Far below them the boy was clawing at his father's legs, trying to climb his way into the embrace, and as the train rocked forward Walenty saw the father raise his right arm as if to—but that was all. The stationmaster's office blocked the view and in an instant there was nothing left to see. Walenty sank down into his seat and closed his eyes. There was no Free State of Trieste and there never could be.

Yours sincerely,
Benjamin R. Ford